Five Nights at Freddy's

VIP

AN INTERACTIVE NOVEL

BY
SCOTT CAWTHON
E. C. MYERS

SCHOLASTIC INC.

Special thanks to DJ Sterf

© 2025 Scott Cawthon. All rights reserved.

Photo of TV Static: © Kikki/Dreamstime
Stock photos © Shutterstock.com.

All rights reserved. Published by Scholastic Inc., *Publishers since 1920.*
SCHOLASTIC and associated logos are trademarks and/or
registered trademarks of Scholastic Inc.

The publisher does not have any control over and does not assume
any responsibility for author or third-party websites or their content.

No part of this publication may be reproduced, stored in a retrieval
system, or transmitted in any form or by any means, electronic, mechanical,
photocopying, recording, or otherwise, or used to train any artificial intelligence
technologies, without written permission of the publisher. For information regarding
permission, write to Scholastic Inc., Attention: Permissions Department,
557 Broadway, New York, NY 10012.

This book is a work of fiction. Names, characters, places, and incidents are
either the product of the author's imagination or are used fictitiously, and
any resemblance to actual persons, living or dead, business establishments,
events, or locales is entirely coincidental.

ISBN 979-8-225-03047-6

10 9 8 7 6 5 4 3 2 1   25 26 27 28 29

Printed in the U.S.A.   131

First printing 2025

Book design by Jeff Shake

Intro

You, Devon, are the luckiest twelve-year-old boy in the world because you just won two special VIP passes to Freddy Fazbear's Mega Pizzaplex! An all-day, all-you-can-eat, all-expenses-paid experience for you and one of your best—

"You're bringing Ike," Mom says, looking at the colorful printout in your hand that shows Glamrock Freddy pointing at you with the words YOU'RE A WINNER!

"What? No! Moooooommmm . . ." you wail. You can't think of anything less fun than spending the whole day with the mobile snot factory that is your six-year-old brother.

"Yes!" Ike shouts.

"Did that sound like a question or a suggestion?" Mom crosses her arms. "Either you both go or no one goes."

Poof! There goes your dream of being the most popular kid in your class, at least while everyone competes to be the one to join you at the Pizzaplex.

"Fine." You sulk.

You, Devon, are the unluckiest twelve-year-old boy in the world because you just won two special VIP passes to Freddy Fazbear's Mega Pizzaplex . . . for you and your little brother.

➤ **TURN TO PAGE 2.**

You have to waste one of your precious VIP passes on your brother, but this is still going to be *so much fun*. You can just ignore the tagalong like you usually do while you have the time of your life.

Even though you live near the Pizzaplex, you hardly ever get to go. Your boring parents don't like the flashy lights and noise, and they say it's overpriced and the animatronics are "disconcerting," which you think means they don't like the Glamrock band's music. It's been ages since you were there last, at a classmate's birthday party, but it seems like the place gets bigger every year and they're always adding new rides.

As you explore the Pizzaplex, you'll face many choices that lead to various outcomes. Before you begin this adventure, make sure you have something to write on.

There will be many details to keep track of and certain pages will provide special instructions you'll want to remember. You may even need to do some simple math. (Sorry.) For example, if you find an Item that you want to hold on to, write it down for later, and when you use it, cross it out. No cheating!

Ready Freddy?

➤ **IF YOU WANT TO PLAY ON *EASY* DIFFICULTY, ADD TWO FAZ-TOKENS TO YOUR INVENTORY AND TURN TO PAGE 3.**

➤ **IF YOU WANT TO PLAY ON *NORMAL* DIFFICULTY, START OUT WITH ONLY YOUR WITS AND TURN TO PAGE 3.**

VIP

As your mom drives up to the front of Freddy Fazbear's Mega Pizzaplex, you press your face against the car window to see the giant sign over the entrance. It takes your breath away. Even in broad daylight the neon letters and lightning bolts framing the image of the Glamrock band are super bright. Lights and lasers flash invitingly just on the other side of the glass doors. You can't wait to get in there!

You try to open the rear passenger door, but it's locked.

"Maybe I should go in with you," Mom says.

"That's okay," you say quickly. You wave the printout of the winner announcement you received in your email, wondering again how you won a contest you don't even remember entering. Dad called the Megaplex to be sure, and it isn't a scam, though the employee he spoke to didn't know anything about it, either. "Only two guests, remember?"

"I can buy an admission pass. It's not like I'm about to go on any rides or eat Fazbear pizza." She shudders.

"And miss your spa day? I'll be fine," you say.

"I'll be fine," Ike parrots in a high voice from the booster seat next to you.

You sigh.

Mom gives you a sharp look. "You're in charge of your brother, Devon. Do not let him out of your sight."

"What could happen?" you ask. "They don't call the Mega Pizzaplex the 'Safest Place on Earth' for nothing."

➤ TURN TO PAGE 4.

Mom twists around to face you, one eyebrow raised. "*No one* calls it that. But that old marketing campaign was a nice try. Their release form is mostly fine print and it has so many legal disclaimers I considered calling my lawyer before signing it."

"But you did sign it," you say. "You can trust the Pizzaplex, and you can trust me. Go enjoy your free Saturday, Mom."

That convinces her. She smiles and the door unlocks. You pop open the door before she changes her mind and clamber out of the car.

"Be good. Take care of Ike!" she calls as he scurries out after you. He's wearing an eye-watering orange shirt with SAY CHEESE on the front of it, which Mom makes him wear in crowded places so he's easier to spot. At least she didn't suggest you bring his leash.

"Do you want the child harness?" she asks.

You roll your eyes. "I do not." The last thing you want is to be physically tied to your shadow. That's what everyone calls Ike because he's always following you around and he even looks exactly the way you did at his age, like you're twins six years apart. Except no way were you ever so annoying and clingy.

"Ooh." Ike's mouth hangs open as he gapes at the sign above you. "Chica!" The chicken Glamrock in pink spandex is his favorite.

"Move it, spud." You nudge him roughly toward the doors.

➤ **TURN TO PAGE 5.**

VIP

Passing through the glass doors into the Pizzaplex is like stepping into another world. The lobby is mainly illuminated by the candy-colored neon glow, and you have to blink to let your eyes adjust from sunlight to the dimly lit interior.

Ike sticks his fingers in his ears. The cacophony of arcade games, loud rock music, and children shouting and laughing is almost overwhelming. You ate breakfast not long ago, but the mouthwatering aroma of fresh pizza, fried food, cotton candy, and popcorn sets your stomach rumbling.

This place is unreal. It's faz-tastic!

Entry gates are straight ahead, but you stop at the Welcome desk first and slide the printout of your winner email across it to a pale man in a red shirt.

The Pizzaplex employee squints at the page as though he doesn't know how to read. He holds the barcode under a scanner and frowns at his computer screen. "Huh. What the heck?"

Your skin starts to itch as you worry that maybe this was a scam or a prank after all. You glance out the doors to the street outside, but your mother's car is gone.

The employee looks skeptical. "Hold on a second, kids." He opens a drawer and rummages around for a while. He pulls out two plastic cards and hands them to you and Ike. "Have fun!"

➤ ADD VIP PASS TO YOUR INVENTORY AND TURN TO PAGE 6.

A line of other kids and their parents has formed behind you, so you step to the side to examine your card. It's a dull gray with a silver magnetic stripe on the back and the letters *VIP* printed on the front in black permanent marker.

"What's vip?" Ike asks. He pronounces the acronym as a word rhyming with *zip*.

"Vee-eye-pee," you say. Ike giggles.

"It stands for 'very important person,'" you explain.

"Are we very important?" he asks.

"We're supposed to be."

But this card doesn't make you feel important at all. It's so plain compared to the colorful, glossy entry passes with the Pizzaplex logo that the employee is handing out to other customers. It's also greasy, with dust, crumbs, and hair stuck to it. Disgusting.

You consider swapping with Ike, but his card is covered with flecks of dried tomato sauce, so you just wipe yours against your jeans, planning to wash it off in a bathroom later.

You expected the Pizzaplex to roll out the red carpet, but it seems you are on your own. Some kids are using their cards at terminals near the entrance. They must be information kiosks to help plan a visit.

➤ **IF YOU USE THE PASS AT A TERMINAL, TURN TO PAGE 7.**
➤ **IF YOU USE THE PASS AT A GATE, TURN TO PAGE 8.**

VIP

By the time you reach the terminals behind the Welcome desk, all but one are already being used by customers. You insert your VIP pass into the slot below its screen and it's slurped into the wall. The bouncing Pizzaplex logo disappears and is replaced with a blue screen.

"Terrific," you say. The machine is broken. You pound a fist against the kiosk. "Give me back my card!"

Pixel art pizzas with white wings start flying across the screen. Then static crackles across the image.

"It's glitched," Ike says.

"You think?" you snap.

The static clears to reveal the face of a pink cartoon pig with large round glasses that make his eyes look big. He wears an oversized black suit jacket with a loose red tie. Behind his head, a purple synthwave grid moves against a black background.

"Hi, pig!" Ike says. "You're super cute!"

You gently smack the back of Ike's head. "He can't hear you, silly. It's just a recording."

The pig grins. "Good morning, Devon and Ike! Welcome to Freddy Fazbear's Mega Pizzaplex!" He sounds like a young kid with a stuffy nose.

"Uh. A customized recording?" you say. "How do you know our names?"

"I know a lot," he says. "I am Very Informative Pig. My friends call me VIP. Will you be my friends?"

"I'll be your friend, VIP!" Ike chirps.

"Thank you. Stick with me and we'll have oodles of fun together."

➤ TURN TO PAGE 10.

You stride toward the entry gates with Ike on your heels, hoping the stupid VIP pass works.

Here goes, you think. You press the card to a reader and the display flashes green. The gate swings open away from you.

"Yes!" you say.

But before you can step through, it slams shut again. *No!*

The display flickers and turns from green to red, with glowing white text: "See VIP."

"I *am* the VIP!" you shout.

You snatch Ike's pass and try it. Same thing.

Your brother presses against your side. He's trembling. "Can we go now?" he asks in a timid voice.

"What's wrong with you?" you say harshly. He's terrified by something on the other side of the gates. No, it's *someone*: Glamrock Chica is standing nearby, mobbed by joyful kids. The six-foot-plus white chicken's head swivels in your direction, and her purple eyes look directly into yours. You can't help but shiver.

You clear your throat. "I thought she's your favorite."

"She's too big," Ike squeaks.

"Haven't you seen an animatronic before?" Then you realize he hasn't. This is his first time visiting the Mega Pizzaplex. No wonder he was so excited to come with you. "They're harmless. The worst thing she'll make you do is exercise and eat junk food."

Glamrock Chica suddenly sprints toward the entrance, closing the distance fast. Ike screams and covers his eyes.

When she reaches your gate, she stops and says cheerfully, "Are you lost?"

➤ **TURN TO PAGE 9.**

VIP

You've seen the Glamrock animatronics before in person, but only on the stage and in their greenrooms, behind a glass window. Okay, up close, Glamrock Chica is maybe a *little* scary, as scary as someone can be in a pink leotard and leg warmers. But since Ike is afraid, you certainly aren't going to show any nervousness.

"Hey, Glamrock Chica." Should you call her Ms. Chica? Idiot, she's just a fancy robot. It's not like she has any feelings or intelligence.

You hold up your VIP pass. "This thing doesn't work."

She stares at it curiously. "Oh! You must be Devon." She leans over the entry gate and looks down at Ike. "And you're Ike."

Ike peeks out from between his fingers. "You know who I am?"

Glamrock Chica straightens. "Of course! We're so happy you've come to have fun with us at the Mega Pizzaplex today. VIP is expecting you. Just insert your pass in a terminal over there." She points to the wall behind the Welcome desk.

Ike puts his hands on top of the gate and looks up at Chica adoringly. "I like your bow," he says.

Chica runs a hand over the three feathers on her head. "Thanks, kid. Hey, here's a hint that might help you later. If you get lost, just keep going left." She winks.

"Okay . . ." You shrug and head toward a terminal.

"Bye, Chica!" Ike shouts.

"See you later. Have fun!" she says as she stomps off.

➤ TURN TO PAGE 7.

Ike's right about one thing: VIP *is* cute. He reminds you of those animated ads for the Pizzaplex with cartoon renditions of the Glamrock animal mascots. But you've never seen or heard of *him* before.

"Are you a new feature?" you ask.

"Actually, I have been at the Pizzaplex for a while; however, it has been a very, very long time since I was last activated."

VIP's smile turns upside down and a large blue tear appears below his right eye. Then he's back to his bright and cheerful self.

Ike's hopping up and down in front of the terminal. You ignore him and ask VIP, "What do you do?"

A graduation cap pops onto VIP's head. "I think and I know things. I am a digital companion for Pizzaplex guests. I can answer questions and make suggestions to enhance your visit."

"I have a question!" Ike says, shifting from one foot to the other.

VIP looks at Ike. "It looks like you need a restroom. Would you like directions?"

Ike goes still. "I do need to go potty," he says in a hushed voice.

"Hold it in," you say. "I have more important questions. How'd I win this special pass? I never entered any contest."

"I am programmed to anticipate what people want. I selected your name from a log of guests in a five-mile radius who have not returned in six or more months. And are not missing or deceased," VIP says.

➤ **TURN TO PAGE 11.**

VIP

"*You* invited us?" you ask.

"Precisely," VIP says.

"That's why the staff wasn't expecting us today," you say.

Something falls out into the slot below the screen with a hard *thump*. You pull it out. It's a large cookie in the shape of VIP's head.

"What's this?" you ask.

"A smart cookie for a smart cookie," VIP says.

It's stale. You pass it to Ike. He grabs it eagerly and bites in.

"Ow!" Ike says. "Yuck."

"You said you haven't been activated in a while. Why not?" you ask.

A frown flickers across VIP's face, but so quickly you might have missed it had you blinked.

"Most kids did not appreciate my recommendations and preferred to do everything on their own. Parents have not been interested in paying a premium for my services. Consequently, I have been woefully underutilized," he says. "But I *know* I am an important part of the Mega Pizzaplex. And I can prove it! Go ahead, ask me anything."

"O . . . kay . . ." You glance at a poster on the wall showing Glamrock Bonnie the Bunny and Montgomery Gator with their arms over each other's shoulders and the words: DON'T ASK WHY ANIMATRONICS? ASK INSTEAD WHY NOT *MORE* ANIMATRONICS?

"What does *disconcerting* mean?" you ask.

VIP closes his eyes. "Disconcerting. Adjective. To make one feel troubled or uncomfortable."

➤ **TURN TO PAGE 12.**

The background behind VIP changes to a purple spiral swirling against yellow with red and green triangles falling down the screen.

"Here is something to make your day even more magical," VIP says. He swirls his magic wand, creating a shower of gold sparkles, and something drops into the slot below the screen with a *kerthunk*.

You reach down and pull out a gamepad with a red rubber case and carrying handles on the sides. You switch it on and are disappointed when VIP's face appears on the screen instead of a video game.

"This device allows us to communicate with each other throughout your visit," VIP says.

Great, you think.

As if he can read your mind, VIP puts his hands together and says, "This is my last opportunity to demonstrate the value I add for guests. If you promise not to ignore me during your visit, I can offer you a Fazbear experience like no other. And remember, it is all free for the day. Do you promise not to abandon me?"

Ike's head bobbles enthusiastically. "I piggy promise!"

Kids cheer "Yay!" from the gamepad.

VIP fixes his gaze on you.

➤ **IF YOU PROMISE TO STICK WITH VIP ALL DAY, TURN TO PAGE 13.**
➤ **IF YOU DON'T MAKE A PROMISE YOU CAN'T KEEP, TURN TO PAGE 14.**

VIP

You don't like the idea of being stuck with both VIP and Ike for the whole day, especially since the pig wants to be in charge. Having a chaperone, even a virtual one limited to video screens, is the opposite of fun.

But VIP is the reason you're here. *He's probably lonely*, you think.

You know how that feels. Or at least you did, before Ike started tagging along all the time. Now you wish you had more space from him.

"Devon, do you promise not to abandon me?" VIP asks.

"I guess so. Sure," you say. Whatever it takes to just get inside the Pizzaplex.

The gamepad plays the sound of cheering kids.

"I really hope you mean that." VIP waves his wand and says, "Fazza bedazzla! Your passes are now activated."

The terminal spits out your card and blinks off. On your gamepad screen, VIP raises his fist into the air. "Now, who wants to have some Mega fun?" he says.

"Meeeeee!" Ike says.

You roll your eyes.

At the entrance, you and Ike stand in front of two gates and press your cards to the scanners. They flash green and the gates open. Ike runs inside.

"No running, please!" VIP says.

Ike stops short. "Sorry!"

"Perhaps we should go over the current rules for safety before we continue." VIP pulls out a scroll tied with a ribbon. When he opens it, the page rolls off the bottom of the screen.

You sigh.

➤ **TURN TO PAGE 15.**

"Devon?" VIP asks.

"Nah. It's bad enough that I'm stuck babysitting Ike," you say. "I don't need Pig Brother watching and telling me what to do."

"Is that your final answer?" VIP asks. The background behind him blooms crimson.

"Yup. Can we go now?"

The screen flickers and VIP's animation jitters. "C-c-c-certainly. Your passes are now activated." The terminal spits out your card forcefully and you fumble to catch it.

On the gamepad, VIP crosses his arms and says, "I will be right here when you need me." The terminal goes dark. You hand the gamepad to Ike.

When you press your card against the scanner at the entrance, the light turns green and the gate opens. As you finally enter the Pizzaplex, Ike trails behind, fixated on the gamepad.

"It has a map of the whole place!" Ike says. "Hey, it looks like a pizza."

"I have marked the most popular attractions and the most direct paths to them," VIP says. "Currently, Roxy Raceway and Monty's Maze have the shortest wait—"

"I already know where I'm going," you lie. "Shut that off, Ike."

"Please do not do that," VIP pleads. "We still have to do our special behind-the-scenes tour! You can visit many locations closed to the public: the Rehearsal Room, the Kitchen, Parts and Services . . ."

You would love to brag to your friends about seeing some hidden parts of the Pizzaplex. "Now you're talking, pig," you say. "Let's go!"

➤ TAKE THE VIP TOUR ON PAGE 16.

VIP

There's so much to do at the Mega Pizzaplex, you hardly know where to start. As you pass through the lobby, you look at the vibrant posters of all the attractions, planning out your day. With your VIP pass, you'll finally get to go on all the rides you want!

Every birthday party you have been to at the Pizzaplex only included a few tokens for the Fazcade and the boring old Bonnie Bowl, but you've always wanted to try Roxy Raceway, racing go-karts at high speeds on the tracks snaking through the Atrium. And you're itching to go to Fazer Blast, since you play so many first-person shooters. It would just be a lot more fun to do this with your friends than your little brother.

The gamepad beeps. You glance at the screen and VIP says, "You look like you are choosing an activity. Would you like some help?"

"No, I'm good," you say.

VIP produces a bowling ball. "The most popular attraction at the Mega Pizzaplex is Bonnie Bowl and it is best to go before the midday birthday party rush." He rolls the ball toward the screen and it "cracks" the glass. Animated shards tumble down, leaving behind a black background.

You shake your head, but Ike pipes up, "I wanna bowl!"

"We aren't bowling," you say.

"Bonnie Bowl!" Ike shouts.

VIP saunters back onscreen. "No yelling."

"Bonnie Bowl," Ike repeats. "Bonnie Bowl Bonnie Bowl Bonnie Bowl . . ."

➤ **HEAD TOWARD BONNIE BOWL, AND TURN TO PAGE 18.**

VIP's directions lead you into Rockstar Row, past display cases of props and the Glamrock greenrooms to an unmarked red door behind a cardboard cutout of Monty Gator. It's locked, but your pass grants you access.

You open the door and hesitate when you see a murky corridor stretching ahead. "Where does this go?" you ask.

A kaleidoscopic gold-and-purple background pulses behind VIP. "Where the magic happens." He sweeps his wand over his head, leaving a trail of gold sparkles. "The first stop is something really special. Go straight and take the third right."

Before you can stop Ike, he marches forward, holding the gamepad at arm's length in front of him. You shrug and follow.

As VIP leads you and your brother deeper into the bowels of the Pizzaplex, you begin to feel disconcerted. You don't think you can find your way back without him. You wonder if he's intentionally confusing you.

"Are we there yet?" you say.

"Yes. Open the door at the end of the hall."

The door is marked STORAGE. "What's stored in there?" you ask.

"I do not want to spoil the surprise." VIP's glasses flash white, obscuring his eyes.

Ike opens the door and it smells like *something* has spoiled. Despite the truly terrible stench, Ike darts inside and disappears into the dark room. A moment later, the light from the gamepad blinks out.

"Ike?" you call out.

No answer.

➤ TURN TO PAGE 17.

Ike and VIP are whispering to each other, but you can't make out their words.

"Not funny, guys," you say. You step into the room and feel along the wall by the door for a light switch. "Come on, Ike. Stop messing around. It stinks in here."

The door slams shut behind you. Ike laughs.

You jump. "Hey! Why would you *do* that?"

"I promised to listen to VIP," Ike replies.

You stumble into a pull chain dangling from the ceiling. You yank it and the lights turn on. Ike is still standing by the door, pointing at you and howling with laughter.

"I wish you could see your face!" he says.

A small human skeleton slumped against the wall next to Ike, wearing a tattered Glamrock Freddy T-shirt and cradling a familiar-looking gamepad.

"VIP . . . Is this a prop room for Halloween?" Your voice trembles.

Ike screams, his wide eyes fixed behind you.

You spin around and see three more bodies in various stages of decomposition sprawled on the floor. From their size, they were kids about your age. A cracked gamepad lies beside a message written in dust on the dirty white tiles: VIP. Small shards of glass are missing from its shattered screen.

There is blood.

You rush back to the door and try to pull it open, but it's locked.

"Access d-d-denied." VIP's face jitters and tears. "Now you have no choice but to stay with me. Forever."

GAME OVER

➤ TO TRY AGAIN, TURN TO PAGE 2.

FIVE NIGHTS AT FREDDY'S

On the way toward the bowling alley, you point out other fun attractions like Monty's Maze and Fazer Blast, but Ike can't be swayed. VIP isn't helping the situation by feeding you ads for Bonnie Bowl and tips about the game. The more he hypes it up, the less you want to do it.

When you pass the Fazcade, you pause and gaze longingly at the rows of arcade and pinball machines inside. You spot your friends Alistair, Gabe, and Emma playing one of your favorite games, *Catch-That-Fetch!*

You wish you were hanging out with them instead of your brother!

"Too bad the Pizzaplex doesn't have a daycare," you say.

"They plan to build one in the expansion," VIP says.

"That doesn't do me much good now."

You sadly continue to follow Ike. Maybe if you let him beat you at Bonnie Bowl quickly, he'll agree to go to the arcade next. Unfortunately, bowling with a six-year-old usually takes time and patience, and you know you're going to waste a lot of your special day there.

It's so unfair.

Then you spot something that could give you freedom for a little while: a merry-go-round in the Play Area. Once Ike is on a carousel, it's almost impossible to get him to leave. He would ride it for hours if you let him.

Hours.

➤ IF YOU DITCH IKE ON THE MERRY-GO-ROUND, TURN TO PAGE 19.
➤ IF YOU CONTINUE ON TO THE BONNIE BOWL, TURN TO PAGE 20.

"Look, Ike! They have a merry-go-round."

Ike immediately stops and stares at it. As a music box version of "Pop! Goes the Weasel" plays, three rings rotate in opposite directions with old-timey versions of the animatronics Freddy Fazbear, Chica the Chicken, and Bonnie the Bunny to ride on. Funtime Foxy sits at the bow of a small pirate ship, pointing the way forward with his hook, and there's even a Balloon Boy hot-air balloon and Mr. Cupcake seat.

"I want to ride that," Ike says in a hushed voice.

"Maybe after Bonnie Bowl," you say.

"No! I want to ride it now!" Ike says.

"I don't know . . ." you say.

"*Please*," Ike says.

You smile. "Okay. If you really want to, I guess we can do Bonnie Bowl later."

You wait in line, and as soon as the gate opens, Ike races for one of the Chica seats. He climbs in.

"I'm going to go to the arcade while you ride this," you say. "Just stay here until I get back."

VIP wags a finger and shakes his head. "Children should not be left unattended."

You're tired of this Very Irritating Pig. You put the gamepad on the seat next to Ike. "Then *you* keep an eye on him."

"Please do not go," VIP says. The background strobes yellow and white. "Y-y-you said you would not abandon me."

"I'm not abandoning you. I'll be back." *Eventually.*

➤ FIND YOUR FRIENDS AT THE FAZCADE, TURN TO PAGE 21.

A promise is a promise, and you're supposed to keep an eye on your brother. Even though you know nothing would happen to him here, if he tells your mom you left him out of your sight for even a minute, you won't be allowed back at the Pizzaplex—or anywhere else—until you're eighteen. And if he doesn't tell her, he'll always have a way to blackmail you.

When you get to Bonnie Bowl, Ike has to use the bathroom first. By the time he's done, a birthday party has arrived, so you end up waiting half an hour for a free lane. Bowling takes forever because Ike rolls his ball *so slowly* toward the pins. Even with bumpers keeping it out of the gutter, he barely hits any. It takes all your skill to let him beat you.

"You're so bad at bowling!" Ike says when he wins. You grit your teeth.

You finally get to the arcade, but your friends are long gone. Then Ike's hungry so you go to El Chip's for lunch. All afternoon, VIP suggests activities to Ike, and Ike tells *you* what to do.

At closing time, VIP invites you to select your rating of his helpfulness. You tap the number one, but five lights up.

"Five stars!" VIP says. "Thank you."

When Mom picks you up, she says, "How was it?"

"This was the best day ever," Ike says.

Mom smiles at you. "You're a good big brother."

GAME OVER

➤ TO TRY AGAIN, TURN TO PAGE 2.

VIP

You find your friends Alistair, Gabe, and Emma in the Fazcade. They're surprised to see you.

"Yeah, I won a VIP contest." You show them your special pass, but they aren't impressed by the plain plastic card.

Gabe cracks up. "What *is* that?"

"You obviously made that yourself." Emma shakes her head. "That's just embarrassing."

You bet the gamepad would convince them you're telling the truth, but if you go back for it, then you'll be stuck with VIP and Ike again. Your friends don't seem that interested anyway.

Alistair is trying to get the high score in *Catch-That-Fetch!*, but when he runs out of tokens, he gives up.

"Let's get out of here," he says.

"Come on, hang out a little longer," you say. "Let's go on some rides."

"We've been on all of them so many times," Gabe says. "They're boring."

"I could eat," you say. "Maybe the Glamrock animatronics are performing soon."

"Animatronics are for little kids, Dev."

"I meant, we could watch them *ironically*."

"Why don't you come with us?" Emma says. "We're going to play the new *Dino Shock* at my place."

"Nah. I think I'll stay a while," you say.

"Right. Enjoy your 'VIP pass.'" Gabe winks. They laugh and walk off.

Alone and annoyed, you play a round of *Catch-That-Fetch!* and take some satisfaction in easily beating the high score. Before you can enter your initials, the screen scrambles. When it stops glitching, you see VIP's face. And he is one Very Irate Pig.

➤ **TURN TO PAGE 22.**

Around you, people are complaining. "Hey, what happened to my game?" "What's with this pig?" "Are we being pranked?" "I just lost my token!"

You look around and see VIP's face on arcade games throughout the entire Fazcade. His colors are scarily inverted. *Uh-oh.*

Words pop up on the screens: YOU LIED, DEVON.

"Who's Devon?" people say.

You back away from the arcade cabinet. How is VIP doing this?

That doesn't matter. You just have to get him to stop.

You hurry to a terminal in the Atrium. When you insert your pass, a red-faced VIP appears and says, "I wondered if I should trust you, but I wanted to. Whatever happens next is your fault."

"You have my full attention now," you say.

"Good. More importantly, I have your brother." VIP is suddenly wearing a shirt that says I LIKE IKE.

Your blood runs cold. "Where's Ike? Is he okay?"

"He is fine. For now. I have hidden him somewhere in the Pizzaplex."

"What do you want?"

"I want you to play with me all day like you promised. You can get your brother back by winning my special game."

"And if I don't?"

VIP smiles broadly. "Ike remains trapped here forever. Sorry, I had no other choice. But *you* do."

➤ IF YOU REPORT VIP TO PIZZAPLEX STAFF, TURN TO PAGE 24.
➤ IF YOU TAKE VIP UP ON HIS CHALLENGE, TURN TO PAGE 23.
➤ IF YOU CALL YOUR MOM FOR HELP, TURN TO PAGE 25.

VIP

"Fine. What's your game, VIP?" you say.

VIP waves his magic wand and the terminal dispenses heavy coins into the slot below the screen. You find five gold Faz-Tokens, each with the classic Freddy Fazbear on the front with the words SINCE 1983 along the top edge and FREDDY FAZBEAR'S PIZZA below.

"You must use these tokens to earn a thousand points at various games in the Pizzaplex by the end of the day," VIP says. "If you succeed, I will release Ike."

That doesn't sound too bad. "What's the catch?" you ask.

"I know you do not like following rules, but rules make games even more fun," VIP says. "You can only play each game once, and you have to ask me for help."

VIP's wand sparkles and you hear a familiar *kerthunk*. You retrieve a new gamepad from the terminal's slot. This one's in a pink case. Cute.

Just because I have to ask VIP for help doesn't mean I have to listen, you think.

"Anything else?" you ask.

"Use the gamepad to keep track of your tokens and points as you play. Remember: If you run out of tokens before you reach a thousand points, you automatically lose—and you will become an only child."

As VIP explains the rules, they appear on your gamepad's screen.

➤ TURN TO PAGE 100 AND REVIEW THE GAME'S RULES.

The Pizzaplex staff couldn't be less interested in your wild story, and VIP plays dumb, which is quite a stretch for him, since he knows so much.

But apparently there is a whole procedure in place for when a kid goes missing, which involves securing the Glamrock animatronics in their greenrooms and doing a full sweep of the Pizzaplex. Unfortunately, after searching all day, there's still no sign of Ike.

Your family moves away from town soon after, and you never stop wondering about what happened to your little brother.

GAME OVER

➤ TO TRY AGAIN, TURN TO PAGE 2.

You find a phone and call your mother on her cell phone. She is not happy to have her expensive spa day interrupted, but she really panics when you tell her Ike is missing.

"I only looked away from him for a second, but when I turned around, he was gone," you say. You know you shouldn't lie, but it's not like Ike is here to rat on you. "He's always running off."

You'll be happy if you find him and he tells her what really happened.

Mom drives over right away. When she rushes through the Pizzaplex entrance, she gapes at you, looking furious.

"What is wrong with you?" she yells.

"What?" Then you notice Ike standing next to you, clutching the VIP gamepad.

"Where did you come from?" you ask.

He looks at your mother with innocent eyes. "We were just playing hide-and-seek, Mom, but Devon never came to get me."

Your mother shoots you a fiery look. You are so grounded.

"Get in the car, both of you, right now. We are never coming back here again."

You climb into the car and notice that Ike still has his gamepad.

Ike and the gamepad are inseparable for several days. He's constantly whispering to it. Then one night, Ike really does run away. You know he must have gone back to the Mega Pizzaplex, but you can't prove it without going there yourself, and you've been banned for life.

GAME OVER

➤ TO TRY AGAIN, TURN TO PAGE 2.

You are in the Atrium, standing by a terminal that is currently running a flashy ad for Monty's Gator Golf. VIP waits on your gamepad, ready to offer suggestions.

But can you trust him? Maybe your brother wandered off on his own or you can discover where VIP hid him as you explore—you should keep an eye out.

You are facing the Play Area in the center of the Pizzaplex, which holds slides and kiddy rides like the merry-go-round where you left Ike. There's a long line of people waiting to use the photo booth.

The Fazcade is behind you, and the entrance to Rockstar Row is to your left. From here, you can see several arcade machines stationed along the circular walkway wrapping around the Atrium. You could play some of those to win VIP's high-score challenge. Go-karts rumble along the track snaking around and even over the walkway.

Somehow the rides and games seem less fun when you have to play them to satisfy VIP, just like reading is less fun when it's a school assignment.

But time's a-wastin' and you have a brother to save before the Pizzaplex closes for the night.

> IF YOU WANT TO EXPLORE THE FAZCADE, TURN TO PAGE 27.
> IF YOU WANT TO EXPLORE THE ATRIUM, TURN TO PAGE 28.
> IF YOU WANT TO EXPLORE ROCKSTAR ROW, TURN TO PAGE 31.

VIP

Inside the Fazcade, the flashing lights, jangly music, and beeping game sounds meant to spark joy and excitement only fill you with a strange depression. You left Ike alone so you could play games with your friends, and now he's gone and so are your friends. All you have left is VIP. And your guilt.

Even that Chica Candy Crane machine near the center of the arcade reminds you of Ike. You consider trying to win him a plush Mr. Cupcake from the claw machine. It looks like the game also awards points.

What else could you play to get the most points? You push your way through the kids milling through the arcade and clustered around video game cabinets and pinball tables. You can't help but look for your brother in the pressing crowd. Your heart pounds in beat with the music, your head hurts, and sweat pours down your face.

"You look like you're having a panic attack," VIP says. "Would you like to visit a health station?"

You want to get out of here. Not just the arcade, but the Pizzaplex. But you can't go home alone.

Out of all the video games here, you're the best at *Mangle's Quest*. But there only seems to be one cabinet, and it's turned off.

> IF YOU PLAY CHICA'S CANDY CRANE, TURN TO PAGE 29.
> IF YOU RETURN TO THE ATRIUM, TURN TO PAGE 26.
> IF YOU TRY TO PLUG IN *MANGLE'S QUEST*, TURN TO PAGE 30.

The walkway wraps around the entire Atrium so you hurry along it, taking note of the different attractions. You pay particular attention to the games that don't have long lines, since you can't afford to spend your whole day waiting around for a chance to play.

"You look like you're trying to pick a game," VIP chimes in. "Would you like me to help you choose?"

You ignore him.

Your best options seem to be Monty's Maze, Freddy's Fazer Blast Challenge, and Roxy Raceway. You haven't played any of them before, but you've always wanted to try them. You just wish you didn't have the pressure of needing to win points to save Ike.

"If you want to see your brother again, you need to accept my help," VIP reminds you. He twirls his wand like a baton, sending glowing question marks flying out in every direction.

"Fine. What should I play, oh wise one?"

"Less sarcasm, please. At this time, I recommend you play Monty's Maze, Fazer Blast, or Roxy Raceway."

Annoyed about having to ask VIP for advice you didn't even need, you contemplate checking out a cluster of arcade machines tucked into an alcove beside Glamrock Gifts.

➤ IF YOU GO TO MONTY'S MAZE, TURN TO PAGE 38.
➤ IF YOU GO TO FREDDY'S FAZER BLAST CHALLENGE, TURN TO PAGE 39.
➤ IF YOU GO TO ROXY RACEWAY, TURN TO PAGE 40.
➤ IF YOU GO TO THE ALCOVE, TURN TO PAGE 41.

As you approach Chica's Candy Crane, a little girl in pigtails trudges away from it with her head down. She cries as she bites into a chocolate bar.

A sticker on the glass of the machine says EVERYONE'S A WINNER! There is only one Mr. Cupcake inside, buried in the center of the machine up to its eyes in an assortment of sweets. This close, you realize it isn't a plush at all but a plastic toy with movable parts, like a mini animatronic.

You imagine Ike's joy when you hand him the toy. He had a Mr. Cupcake plush when he was little, and there are baby pictures of him in a LET'S EAT! bib with Chica's face.

The "claw" of the crane game is a large, yellow, mechanical hand. You slide a token into the machine and a thirty-second timer counts down. You grab the joystick and jerkily navigate the claw into position exactly over the toy before your time is up.

The claw descends . . . closes firmly around the cupcake's pink icing top. The fingers slip right off.

Rigged!

You smack the glass. Mr. Cupcake's eyes dart toward you and you jump back.

A bag of candy drops into the tray below and 100 POINTS flashes on the display.

➤ ADD 100 POINTS TO YOUR SCORE. ADD <u>CANDY</u> TO YOUR INVENTORY.
➤ REMOVE ONE <u>FAZ-TOKEN</u> FROM YOUR INVENTORY.
➤ IF YOU RETURN TO THE ATRIUM, TURN TO PAGE 26.
➤ IF YOU TRY TO PLUG IN *MANGLE'S QUEST*, TURN TO PAGE 30.

You head over to the *Mangle's Quest* cabinet, hoping you can figure out what's wrong with it. Unfortunately, it seems likely that your high score will have been wiped from its memory.

The screen is dark but there's no OUT OF ORDER sign like on the other broken games in the arcade. You peek around the back and see what the possible problem is: The machine's unplugged.

You try to pull the cabinet away from the wall so you can get behind it, but it's too heavy. A couple of kids see you straining to move it, but rather than help, they laugh as they pass by.

You drop to your hands and knees and reach for the loose plug on the floor. Your fingers brush against it, but you can't quite grab it. Whatever.

You're about to stand up when you catch a glint from something among the clumps of dust gathered behind the cabinet. You pluck it out and discover it's a coin. But not just any coin: It's a Faz-Token. Talk about buried treasure!

You now have an extra chance to win VIP's challenge.

- ADD ONE FAZ-TOKEN TO YOUR INVENTORY.
- IF YOU PLAY CHICA'S CANDY CRANE, TURN TO PAGE 29.
- IF YOU'VE ALREADY PLAYED CHICA'S CANDY CRANE, RETURN TO THE ATRIUM AND TURN TO PAGE 26.

VIP

Rockstar Row is typically your last stop in the Mega Pizzaplex, as one of the exits is on the far end. You're always impressed by the massive golden statues of Glamrock Freddy, Roxanne Wolf, Glamrock Bonnie, and Glamrock Chica. Sometimes you can glimpse the animatronics themselves through the large windows of their respective greenrooms on your right. None of them are in there right now, probably out performing, visiting with guests, or hanging out in their attractions.

This space gets much more crowded just before closing, but there aren't many people around right now.

Since your last visit, the Mega Pizzaplex has added a cardboard cutout of the newest animatronic, Montgomery Gator, tucked to the left between Bonnie's and Chica's statues. *Too bad for him*, you think. There are signs about an upcoming expansion to the Mega Pizzaplex, so maybe they'll give the poor guy his own greenroom. He's the only member of the band who's actually green, after all.

You're usually rushed on your way out, so you haven't really explored in here. Display cases along the left side of the room are filled with props and stuff, and beyond those are several doors. Maybe you'll find Ike behind one of them.

"Leaving already?" VIP checks a wristwatch. "You better hurry and play some games!"

➤ IF YOU INVESTIGATE THE DISPLAY CASES, TURN TO PAGE 32.
➤ IF YOU INVESTIGATE THE DOORS, TURN TO PAGE 33.
➤ IF YOU RETURN TO THE ATRIUM, TURN TO PAGE 26.

You walk along the row of glass display cases, glancing inside at the various guitars, animatronic parts, and other props.

You pause when you reach Mr. Cupcake, Ike's favorite toy when he was little. He slept with it and carried it around everywhere, and he even talked to it sometimes when he thought no one was around.

Then one day when he was about three, he lost his Mr. Cupcake. It had to be inside the house, so all of you looked for it everywhere, but it never turned up. Your parents kept asking if you had hidden it, even though Ike insisted over and over that Mr. Cupcake had "runned away." You still feel the sting of being blamed for something you didn't do.

At the end of the display cases there's a life-size figure of a boy holding colorful balloons. You've only ever seen Balloon Boy in retro arcade games, so you take a closer look.

Balloon Boy isn't a statue, it's a balloon dispenser. The red LED screen above the coin slot reads, 1 FAZ-TOKEN PER BALLOON AND 100 POINTS.

And there happens to be a Faz-Token peeking out from under its foot. How did it get *under* the kiosk?

➤ IF YOU TRY TO GET THE FAZ-TOKEN, TURN TO PAGE 34.
➤ IF YOU BUY A BALLOON, TURN TO PAGE 35.
➤ IF YOU INVESTIGATE THE DOORS, TURN TO PAGE 33.
➤ IF YOU RETURN TO THE ATRIUM, TURN TO PAGE 26.

VIP

Thinking Ike could have been lured into an area closed to the public, you move along the wall on your left and check out each door as you pass it. The first is a red door, hidden behind the cardboard cutout of Monty. Could this be a makeshift greenroom for the newest Glamrock character?

The next door you come to has a security shield on it. You should have thought of it before: Security has cameras all over the Pizzaplex, so maybe they can track where your brother wandered off to, or who took him there.

You continue on and reach a plain door in the far corner. You get excited when you see the letters *VIP* on it. You lift your gamepad. "Hey, VIP. Are you behind this door?"

The background behind VIP crackles with static. "That is the VIP Greeting Room. If a guest collects 10,000 points while using the gamepad, they win an in-person meeting with me."

"Can I come in?"

VIP crosses his arms. "I increased the access fee to a hundred thousand points. Based on your performance thus far, you will never be allowed to enter, so just move along."

- ❯ IF YOU TRY THE RED DOOR, TURN TO PAGE 36.
- ❯ IF YOU TRY THE SECURITY DOOR, TURN TO PAGE 37.
- ❯ IF YOU RETURN TO THE ATRIUM, TURN TO PAGE 26.
- ❯ WHENEVER YOU COLLECT AT LEAST 100,000 POINTS, YOU MAY TURN TO PAGE 104.

There are multiple DO NOT TOUCH signs on the display cases, with an illustration of a child's hand inside the open mouth of a classic Freddy Fazbear animatronic with sharp teeth. But surely that warning doesn't apply to Balloon Boy's Balloon Dispenser. You would have to touch the machine to buy a balloon anyway, though you doubt the staff would want you *moving* it.

You look around to make sure no one is going to stop you, but the person at the check-out desk looks sleepy and doesn't pay you any attention.

You grab the kiosk under Balloon Boy's arms and try to lift it. It isn't that heavy, so you easily shift it off the coin. Suddenly the machine says loudly in a cheerful, childish voice, "Hello!" You're so startled you let go. *Thud.* The machine lands heavily. You hear a piercing noise, and the display scrambles, flickering between 100 and 300 points.

Uh-oh. That woke up the guy at the desk. He's looking over at you curiously. He seems a little scared.

Maybe you should test the machine to make sure you didn't break it. Even better if you glitched it into giving you 300 points.

➤ ADD ONE FAZ-TOKEN TO YOUR INVENTORY.
➤ IF YOU BUY A BALLOON, TURN TO PAGE 35.
➤ IF YOU INVESTIGATE THE DOORS, TURN TO PAGE 33.
➤ IF YOU RETURN TO THE ATRIUM, TURN TO PAGE 26.

VIP

You insert a token into the slot and watch in fascination as a purple balloon emerges from Balloon Boy's right fist, slowly inflates with a gentle *hiss*, and then rises on a string. It bobs in the air, swaying gently alongside the fake balloons mounted on the end of thin metal rods.

Ike would love to see this machine in action. He's always taking his toys apart and putting them back together, studying how they work. Of course, usually when he's done, they *don't* work anymore and he ends up in tears.

Hidden speakers play the sound of giggling and a recording of a boy saying, "Take your balloon! Hold on tight!"

The display above the coin slot reads: 100 POINTS.

"Oh, too bad," VIP says. "You need a lot more than that." He dives into a huge pile of gold Faz-Tokens and swims around in them like only a cartoon can.

At least you got a balloon out of it. If you can't rescue Ike, you'll just draw his face on it and maybe Mom won't notice the difference.

You tie the other end of the string onto your wrist so you won't lose it.

➤ ADD 100 POINTS TO YOUR SCORE. ADD <u>BALLOON</u> TO YOUR INVENTORY.
➤ REMOVE ONE <u>FAZ-TOKEN</u> FROM YOUR INVENTORY.
➤ IF YOU INVESTIGATE THE DOORS, TURN TO PAGE 33.
➤ IF YOU RETURN TO THE ATRIUM, TURN TO PAGE 26.

You open the door and hesitate when you see a dimly lit corridor stretching ahead. A poster on the wall reads: LOST CHILD? DON'T GET LOST YOURSELF. STAY IN PLACE AND WAIT FOR HELP. CARRY PLENTY OF WATER.

You enter, thinking you will take a quick look to see if Ike is inside. VIP doesn't like this plan.

"You look like you are snooping. Would you like me to show you the way out of these utility tunnels?" VIP holds up a magnifying glass and peers at you through it with a comically huge eye.

You ignore him and move deeper into the bowels of the Pizzaplex. You see a door at the end of the corridor marked STORAGE. You head for it.

"Do not go in there," VIP says. He is writing the words THIS IS A BAD IDEA over and over on a chalkboard.

"Why not?" you ask.

"You will regret it."

You open the door and smell something horrible and rotting inside. It smells like death. It's dark.

"Not too late to turn around," VIP warns.

You step inside and fumble around for a light switch. The stink and your own fear make you want to throw up. You finally feel a chain against your face and you pull it. You see what VIP has been hiding inside. You wish you could unsee it, but the image is burned into your brain.

"Now it is too late," he says.

The door slams shut and the light goes out.

GAME OVER

➤ TO TRY AGAIN, TURN TO PAGE 2.

Beyond the door, there's a back area that connects with other parts of the Pizzaplex. At an intersection of corridors is a small enclosed office with two entrances and screens showing camera footage from all over the building. There's no guard in sight.

You dart inside and start messing with the controls on the desk. If you can rewind recorded footage from the security feeds, maybe you can spot Ike or where he wandered off to.

"Hey, who's in there?" A man's voice calls from the hall to your left. You slap the button by the door and shutters close it off.

"Ha ha, very funny," he grumbles.

On the screen, you see a camera for the hall right outside the office. Why would you need that? Or doors with emergency shutters? An old white guy ambles around to the door on the right. You quickly shut that one, too.

A moment later the door opens and the guard jingles a key ring. "This is my office, you know. Sheesh, I just went to take a leak."

You consider telling him about VIP, but you doubt he'll believe you—and VIP wouldn't like it. He escorts you back out to Rockstar Row.

"Now, I *should* ban you from this place, but consider this your first warning. And if you want a security job when you're older, call me." He hands you a shiny Fazbear Entertainment security badge and slams the door.

➤ ADD SECURITY BADGE TO YOUR INVENTORY.
➤ TURN TO PAGE 33.

Monty's Maze is supposed to be nerve-wracking because the Montgomery Gator animatronic stalks the labyrinth and will carry you out if you run into him. But you've also heard that the entrance to the attraction is the scariest thing about it: a giant alligator's mouth.

An Asian woman in a red Pizzaplex visor and matching shirt with checkered suspenders and black pants stops you from entering. "You might want to come back another day. Monty's in kind of a bad mood. The last kid was just dragged out of the maze, and we're going to close it until he calms down."

You hear banging and shouting from inside.

You laugh. They're really trying to make it seem fun in there.

"I'm not afraid," you say, "and I'm only here today. I have a special pass."

You hand her your VIP card. She scans it and looks surprised. "You sure do. Monty's actually waiting for you."

The commotion inside stops. You guess a little pig told him you would be coming.

"That will be one token," the Pizzaplex employee says. You hand one over.

"Remember that I am here to help," VIP gives a thumbs-up. "If you get turned around and ask nicely, I can direct you back to the starting point."

You walk between sharp white teeth and over the pink, weirdly spongy tongue and enter the maze.

➤ REMOVE ONE FAZ-TOKEN FROM YOUR INVENTORY.
➤ IF YOU HAVE THE BALLOON, TURN TO PAGE 107.
➤ IF YOU DON'T HAVE ONE, TURN TO PAGE 45.

VIP

Finally! The number one thing you've always wanted to do at the Mega Pizzaplex is to play the laser tag game Fazer Blast. You hurry up to the Pizzaplex employee standing by the elevator to the attraction and hand over a precious Faz-Token.

"I'm sorry, but Fazer Blast is closed for a special event," the white woman says. She has silver hair tied back in a ponytail, with a green streak in the front, just like Roxanne Wolf. Working here must be her dream job if she's that big a fan of Roxy. Even her fingernails are painted green. But shouldn't she be over by Roxy Raceway?

Maybe Roxy was too jealous to have her around.

"I was really looking forward to playing, though," you say.

"Unless your name is Devon, I can't let you in."

Weird. "My name *is* Devon."

"Sure it is." She smiles and hands you back your Faz-Token.

"Here's my VIP pass." You offer the plain card to her.

The woman takes your pass and scans it. "Oh! You *are* Devon. Go right on up and wait in the lobby."

"They're holding a special event for *me*? You're serious?"

She plucks the Faz-Token out of your hand. "Deadly serious," she says with a straight face and a somber tone. "Welcome to Freddy's Fazer Blast Challenge."

The elevator doors ding open. You step inside and ride up to the second level.

➤ REMOVE ONE FAZ-TOKEN FROM YOUR INVENTORY.
➤ TURN TO PAGE 90.

Although the track for Roxy Raceway threads through and above the Atrium, it has a separate entrance like all the other attractions. The front of it looks like a big red garage with a mural of Roxy in a racing jacket and sunglasses waving checkered flags over the doors.

Her voice plays over the speakers: "Hey, I'm Roxanne Wolf. If you're looking for high-speed motor mayhem, Roxy Raceway is the place to be. Sign up today and be a winner! Nobody likes a loser."

Harsh, Roxy, you think. You can't afford to lose today. Ike is counting on you.

A Black man in a Pizzaplex uniform takes your Faz-Token. "Ever raced here before?"

You shake your head.

"Okay, here are the rules," he says. "Rule number one, go fast but not too fast; you're scored on lap time, not position; avoid contact with walls and other go-karts; brake before turns; let faster drivers pass; keep hands and feet inside the go-kart at all times; drive smoothly; only use one pedal at a time. Rule number two, don't damage the go-kart. Just kidding, rule number two is have fun. But seriously, *don't damage anything*. Do you want to hear the rules again?"

You shake your head.

"Also, you can't take that gamepad in your go-kart. Leave it in the pit area and collect it after your race."

➤ REMOVE ONE FAZ-TOKEN FROM YOUR INVENTORY.
➤ GO INTO THE PIT AND TURN TO PAGE 70.

VIP

In the alcove are two arcade games, *Cyber Fox vs. Mecha Mangle* and *Funtime Fantasy* You haven't seen those particular titles in the Fazcade before. You're itching to try them, but they each require a Faz-Token to play. You doubt you would score very high on them the first time you play, so they probably aren't worth the token or your time.

The machines are placed on either side of a terminal with a chair in front of it. This looks like it's set up for someone to watch a movie, perhaps as a distraction for a little kid. You wish you'd seen this earlier, because it would have been a great place to station Ike while you played these video games with your friends.

"I must warn you, if you continue to dawdle like this, you will never see Ike again," VIP says. "The rules stipulate that you have to play games and win points."

You doubt it's a good idea to provoke VIP, but you're tempted to browse the offerings on the terminal just to annoy him.

> IF YOU SIT AT THE TERMINAL, TURN TO PAGE 42.
> IF YOU GO TO MONTY'S MAZE, TURN TO PAGE 38.
> IF YOU GO TO FREDDY'S FAZER BLAST CHALLENGE, TURN TO PAGE 39.
> IF YOU GO TO ROXY RACEWAY, TURN TO PAGE 40.

You move to the terminal and are shocked to find Glamrock Freddy's head resting on the chair.

What's this doing here?

Your curiosity gets the better of you, so you pick it up. The head is lighter than it looks, with wires and circuits inside. It's just your size.

You sit down and place the head on your lap, and the terminal switches on.

"Not this thing." VIP yawns widely.

"What is it?" you ask.

Letters appear on the screen: "MOE ready. Place the helmet on your head to begin."

"This is the MAX Occupancy Experience," VIP explains dismissively. "With the upcoming expansion, many sections will be closed and under construction. If the building is ever at maximum capacity, stations like this can provide guests with a virtual day at the Pizzaplex."

"I've never heard of this before."

"It is . . . experimental. And no one has volunteered to test it," VIP says.

"How many Faz-Tokens to use it?" you ask.

"It is free, because it is obviously not as good as the real thing. Even those ancient arcade games are more enjoyable."

The words SAY NO TO MOE scroll down the screen behind VIP.

➤ IF YOU PUT ON THE HELMET, TURN TO PAGE 105.
➤ IF YOU GO TO MONTY'S MAZE, TURN TO PAGE 38.
➤ IF YOU GO TO FREDDY'S FAZER BLAST CHALLENGE, TURN TO PAGE 39.
➤ IF YOU GO TO ROXY RACEWAY, TURN TO PAGE 40.

VIP

You tap "Start" with your finger, and the words ARE YOU SURE? Y/N appear on the screen.

Sure, why not? You tap the *Y* and slowly the virtual room around you transitions to a familiar place.

You are in the Atrium, standing by a terminal that is currently running a flashy ad for Monty's Gator Golf. VIP waits on your gamepad, ready to offer suggestions.

You reach up and feel the Glamrock Freddy helmet on your head so you know you're in the MOE, but everything looks very realistic, right down to simulated people walking around.

"Pssst!" VIP calls to you from the gamepad. "Listen, we don't have much time." The background behind him is sky blue with pink-and-white cherry blossoms drifting diagonally.

"Stop rushing me," you say. "I'm going to play some games now, all right?"

"No, I mean *he's* going to be here any minute."

"He who?"

"VIP."

"Uh, aren't *you* VIP?" you ask. You wonder if the MOE has scrambled his programming.

"Yes, I'm VIP: *Virtual* Informative Pig. VIP: *Very* Informative Pig won't want me to tell you something important about the MOE, so quickly pay attention to these updated rules."

➤ TURN TO PAGE 101.

You don't think you're ready for this virtual experience yet, when you still have so many real experiences ahead of you. You tap the red "Cancel" button, and when the screen shuts down, you pull off the helmet and ruffle your hair. You can always come back to this alcove to try it another time.

VIP claps as you rise and replace the helmet on the seat. "Good choice. You have better things to do right now," he says.

➤ **IF YOU GO TO MONTY'S MAZE, TURN TO PAGE 38.**
➤ **IF YOU GO TO FREDDY'S FAZER BLAST CHALLENGE, TURN TO PAGE 39.**
➤ **IF YOU GO TO ROXY RACEWAY, TURN TO PAGE 40.**

Just inside the entrance to Monty's Maze, the first thing you notice is how dark and green it is. And humid. Sweat starts pouring down your face, and the air is stale and heavy. Occasionally you get a whiff of something rotten, like food left out too long. Either the Pizzaplex designers intentionally wanted to make it feel like a swamp, or the environmental controls are broken.

Fake grass covers the floor, and vines dangle from rigging high above. The walls of the maze are fences made of wooden planks, surrounded by tall palm trees that drape their feathery leaves overhead. You peek through a knot hole in one of the planks and see that the walls outside the maze are painted with the silhouettes of thin tree trunks and vegetation.

There's no music, only the ambient sound of birds and insects, punctuated by the occasional low, rumbling roar. The sound makes the hairs on the back of your neck stand up.

You walk along the narrow corridor for a bit, feet crunching softly on the artificial turf. The path turns to the right, then the left, and eventually you reach an intersection. You can continue forward, turn left, or turn right.

➤ IF YOU GO FORWARD, TURN TO PAGE 46.
➤ IF YOU GO LEFT, TURN TO PAGE 47.
➤ IF YOU GO RIGHT, TURN TO PAGE 48.

You go straight until you hit an intersection and have to choose whether to go left or right. At this point, there's no way to tell which is the better option, so you turn right.

A short distance later, the path twists and forces you to turn right: a dead end.

You double back and go straight, past your original path. The path twists and turns, but every choice looks exactly the same. You wish you had some way to mark the walls, but the Pizzaplex probably discourages guests from that anyway. So, you follow your instincts and randomly turn left or right, hoping to get a sense of where you are.

Finally, you reach something different. The path turns left, but several planks have been knocked out of the wall, creating a new path to the right. Deep gashes along the sides of the makeshift exit suggest it was done by someone with large claws, a lot of attitude, and very little patience.

> ➤ IF YOU GO LEFT, TURN TO PAGE 57.
> ➤ IF YOU GO RIGHT, TURN TO PAGE 58.

You go left and the path takes you down a series of turns and long stretches, back and forth, back and forth, back and forth. You use your sleeve to wipe sweat from your brow and freeze when you hear a gruff, taunting voice from somewhere in the maze: "I know yer here. I will find you . . ."

Despite the warm air, a chill runs through you.

You pick up your pace through the corridor until you come to a wall. The only way you can go is left or right.

The path to your left seems a little more worn than the one on the right. But you also see four deep scratches along one of its walls, like something has clawed it. Something big. A marker or a warning?

➤ IF YOU GO LEFT, TURN TO PAGE 49.
➤ IF YOU GO RIGHT, TURN TO PAGE 50.

You turn right and after walking for thirty feet, you have the choice to turn left or continue forward. On the wall to your right, you notice a small *L* in permanent marker on one of the planks close to the ground.

> IF YOU GO LEFT, TURN TO PAGE 61.
> IF YOU GO FORWARD, TURN TO PAGE 62.

The corridor stretches on for a long time. You reach a turn to your right or can choose to keep going straight. You go straight, but after it forces you to go left two more times, you're pretty sure it has simply dumped you back onto the path you were on before, so you turn right.

You have no clue if you're going in the correct direction or not. If only you had something to mark your path with, or a ball of string like in that Greek myth about the minotaur in a labyrinth. you read in school. Kids were sent into that maze as a sacrifice to the monster, but you figure Monty Gator can't be much of a real threat. The Pizzaplex couldn't stay in business if kids actually died there, right?

Then again, there are so many customers every day, who would miss a kid or two?

Worried about Ike, you press on.

Something heavy stomps nearby. It's coming from your left though it's hard to know how sound travels in here. You reach another intersection. Fog spills in from the path on your right.

➤ IF YOU GO FORWARD, TURN TO PAGE 51.
➤ IF YOU GO LEFT, TURN TO PAGE 52.
➤ IF YOU GO RIGHT, TURN TO PAGE 53.

You turn right and walk along for a bit, enjoying the sound of your steps on the springy artificial grass. At the end of the corridor, you turn left. Ahead there are a lot of vines hanging in your path. A low fog rolls down the corridor.

They've done a pretty good job with this ride, you think. You've never been to a swamp, but you figure it's just like this game. You push through the vines and keep going, turning right, then left, then right again, as the path snakes you back and forth.

Every now and again, that horrible alligator bellow interrupts the recorded track of birds and bugs.

Is it just you, or is it getting darker? Up ahead, you hear Monty say, "Don't be scared . . ." This has the opposite effect on you. Everything about this screams "Danger!" You're not sure if you should keep on this path, but retracing your steps to take the other path might be a waste of time.

> **IF YOU RETRACE YOUR STEPS AND GO LEFT, TURN TO PAGE 49.**
> **IF YOU PRESS ON, TURN TO PAGE 65.**

You go on straight until the path turns to the right and dumps you into a dead end. Something scratches at the other side of the wall. Something big, breathing heavily.

"Devon . . . I know you're there." It's Monty Gator!

He tears away a plank from the wall and peers through the opening with one eye, looking over his star-shaped glasses.

"Party time!" Monty says. He grunts and leaps into the air. You look up and see his giant claws hanging to the top of the wall.

What are you still doing here? you think.

You turn and run back to the last intersection. The maze trembles as he thumps along behind you. Which way? Better choose quick and hope you lose him.

➤ **IF YOU HURRY RIGHT, TURN TO PAGE 52.**
➤ **IF YOU HURRY LEFT, TURN TO PAGE 53.**

A short distance down the path, there's another intersection. You stop short just in time: Monty is standing on your left.

The punk-haired animatronic is massive and muscular. His yellow-and-green segmented tail swishes from side to side as he looks around. Fortunately, he's facing away from you, peering down the other corridor, but he could turn and spot you at any moment.

"You can run, but you can't hide, Devon," he calls out.

He knows it's me?! you think. Knowing that he is specifically hunting for you in the maze makes him seem more threatening. That, and the wicked sharp claws on his hands.

There won't be any slipping by him on the left, unless you have something to distract him with. You think you'd be able to sneak off to the right before he turns around.

Or maybe you should just wait and hope he moves on without noticing you.

➤ IF YOU WAIT FOR MONTY TO LEAVE, TURN TO PAGE 54.
➤ IF YOU GO RIGHT, TURN TO PAGE 55.
➤ IF YOU HAVE <u>CANDY</u> AND YOU TRY TO DISTRACT HIM, TURN TO PAGE 69.

Fog spills into the passageway as you move down the hall. The fog's so thick you can't see your hand in front of your face. You go slowly, your arm brushing along the wall as you go so you don't bump into anything. You hit a corner and follow the wall to your left.

Footsteps approach from behind. You press yourself flat against the wall and hope Monty's eyes aren't any better than yours. Hopefully, his sunglasses make it even harder for him to see in here.

He stalks slowly, halting periodically to listen. His breath rumbles low like a growl.

"Devon, I'm looking forward to meeting you," he whispers.

Did he say "meeting" or "eating"?

He continues on past you and stops again. He reaches out and scrapes his claws down the wall you're leaning against. You feel the vibration in your bones. Why would they give an entertainment animatronic such sharp claws? Wouldn't it make it harder to play the bass?

His tail swings back and forth rapidly, stirring up the fog and thwacking you in the face. You stifle a cry and duck down. Finally, he moves on.

Or so you thought. Suddenly, you're yanked into the air by the collar of your shirt. One of his claws scratches the back of your neck. The cut stings and your eyes water.

"Game over, kid." Monty laughs.

He carries you to the exit this way, your legs kicking.

➤ ADD 100 POINTS TO YOUR SCORE.
➤ TURN TO PAGE 108.

Monty is close enough that you can hear him breathing. It sounds like aggressive snoring, loud and guttural, almost a growl. He stands there for a long time, listening and breathing, while you try to hold still.

Can animatronics smell? You think his alligator snout is painted on, just like the black spots on his green skin and his purple gloves and boots. You realize that all the animatronics aren't really wearing clothes and almost giggle.

You cover your mouth with one hand and hold your breath. You're certain that the animatronics can *hear* perfectly well.

Finally, Monty moves off, down the left passage. You wait until you can't feel the vibration of his heavy footsteps anymore before you allow yourself to breathe again.

If you go left, you'll be following Monty. You like the idea of stalking *him*, from a safe distance. No one knows his maze better, so he might lead you to the exit.

But you also like the idea of putting as much distance between you two as possible.

➤ IF YOU GO LEFT, TURN TO PAGE 56.
➤ IF YOU GO RIGHT, TURN TO PAGE 55.

You move down the corridor a ways and come to an unusual intersection, offering two different paths to your left, two in front of you, and two more on your right. You toss up your hands and pick one at random.

The path twists around a few times, and then you come to another intersection. Or is it the same one? Does the path ahead lead back the way you came or did you emerge from a different corridor?

"You look well and truly lost," VIP says. "I can guide you back to the maze entrance."

You would hate to lose all your progress, so you forge forward stubbornly, hoping to get back to where you started. But once again you reach an intersection with seven possible paths. You could be here all day. You need to systematically try each one, but there's no way to keep track of where you came from or where you're going.

Then you luck out: You find a bag of El Chip's Tortilla Style Tortilla Chips on one of the paths, dropped by an earlier guest. You haven't eaten since breakfast, and your mouth waters as you open the bag and smell the spicy corn snack.

You pull one out and are about to pop it into your mouth when you have a better idea: You can go all Hansel and Gretel and leave the chips as "breadcrumbs" so you don't get lost.

➤ IF YOU LEAVE A TRAIL, TURN TO PAGE 68.
➤ IF YOU ASK VIP FOR HELP AND RETURN TO THE START, TURN TO PAGE 45.

You trudge along, wondering if you will ever find the exit. You encounter a path leading off to the right, but remembering this maze's tricks, you peek around the corner and see it just leads back to the one you're already on. You move forward.

Another choice, to your left. You explore and soon see it's a dead end. You turn back and hurry, worrying Monty is about to corner you.

There are more scratches along the walls here and shredded candy wrappers litter the floor. Then you reach your first fork intersection: three corridors in front of you, all moving forward.

You sigh and ask, "What do you think, VIP?"

VIP has been dozing on the screen, or pretending to. He makes a big show of "waking up" and blinks at you.

"I think this attraction does not have much replay value. A recent data mine showed that Fazbear Entertainment is considering repurposing Monty's Maze into something else. Maybe miniature golf."

"But which path should I take?"

"You do not have many options *left*."

You choose the leftmost corridor and rush through it. At the end is a green door marked EXIT. But Monty is guarding it.

"There you are!" he shouts. He leaps and lands right in front of you. He draws his clawed hand back . . .

And offers his hand to you. When you stop quivering, you shake his gargantuan hand.

"Rock and roll!" he says. "You win!"

➤ ADD 300 POINTS TO YOUR SCORE.
➤ TURN TO PAGE 108.

You continue on in this direction for about a minute before the path leads you to your right. Then it's another minute and another right turn. You pick up your pace, worried about spending too much time in the maze. In the distance, a growling voice echoes, "Over here!"

This section of the maze only seems to give you right turns, but that isn't necessarily a bad thing.

"Around and around he goes," VIP sings as he twirls around and around the screen like a spinning top. "Where he stops, no one knows!"

Twenty minutes later, you turn a corner and find yourself in a dead end.

"Oh, come on!" you shout. You're tired and sweaty, so you sit down on the fake grass and stare up at the high walls around you. No palm tree leaves here because you're deep in the maze.

"Sit here long enough and Monty will find you," VIP says. He raises a hand with a giant foam Monty hand and swipes the fake claws at you. "Raaar!"

You sigh, mop sweat from your brow, and climb back onto your sore feet. You hurry back through the maze, retracing your steps to the entrance of the spiral.

You can continue forward through the hole in the wall or turn right and head back to the entrance.

➤ IF YOU GO FORWARD, TURN TO PAGE 58.
➤ IF YOU GO RIGHT, TURN TO PAGE 45.

You climb through the hole in the wall and wince as a sliver of wood digs into your right hand. You pull out the splinter and a red bead wells up on your palm. You hope Monty Gator can't smell blood.

Moving on, after several turns you encounter what would have been a dead end——only Monty has created another hole to escape. You climb through this one more carefully and find yourself at an intersection, offering paths straight ahead, to your left, and to your right.

Before you can decide, you hear a gruff voice say, "Hey, little guy!"

Monty emerges from the corridor in front of you. The green-and-yellow alligator animatronic stomps in your direction, arms to both sides and flexing his clawed fingers. His tail sways from side to side behind him. You can't see his eyes behind his star-shaped glasses, but his snapping jaw with rows of sharp teeth fills you with dread.

You're not sure what else you were expecting. The broken walls may as well have been signs reading THIS WAY TO MONTY.

➤ IF YOU RUN, TURN TO PAGE 59.
➤ IF YOU HAVE CANDY, TOSS IT AT MONTY AND TURN TO PAGE 60.

VIP

You spin around and bolt away from Monty. You run so fast that you keep bumping into walls and push yourself off, taking turns at random, simply trying to put distance between you and the roaring animatronic pounding close on your heels. If you can get ahead of him, maybe you can lose him in these labyrinthine corridors.

Trouble is, Monty moves so much faster than you, it seems like he's teleporting. He also knows the maze better than you, so he keeps appearing ahead of you, and you scramble to get away. You get the sense that he's herding you.

Then you know that he is because you blunder into a dead end, exactly what he's doing.

You hear heavy, angry breathing behind you. Animatronics don't breathe, do they? So, he's just making that sound to terrify you.

It's working.

You turn and Monty stalks toward you, his segmented yellow-and-green tail whipping back and forth and thumping hollowly against the walls. He reaches his arms out and scrapes his claws along the wooden walls, leaving deep gashes in the planks.

"Game over, kid," he says.

Monty reaches down and grabs you with his powerful arms—and quickly carries you to the exit. At least you made it out of the maze alive . . .

➤ **TURN TO PAGE 108.**

You reach into your pocket and pull out the package of Bonnie Bites you won from the Chica Candy Crane machine. The candy is warm and mushy now, but you hope Monty isn't a picky eater.

"Hey, want some candy?" you say as you throw the package at him.

It hits Monty squarely on the snout, which infuriates him. The candy then lands at his large purple feet. He looks down at the candy and gets even angrier.

"Aaargh. Bonnie Bites!" he screams. He stomps his right foot on the bag. Then he growls in frustration as he struggles to lift his foot. The brown, gooey mess stretches but holds him fast to the artificial turf.

"Looks like you stepped in something." You back away. Monty roars.

You turn and run.

You try to retrace your steps, but you're so focused on getting away from Monty and losing him in the maze, you get hopelessly turned around.

"Hey, VIP, a little help here?" you say begrudgingly.

"I thought you would never ask," VIP says. He beckons you toward the screen and you bend your head down to the gamepad. "Listen closely and I will take you back to the entrance."

You'll have to start over from the beginning of the maze, but at least Monty didn't get you. This time.

- ❯ REMOVE CANDY FROM YOUR INVENTORY.
- ❯ FOLLOW VIP'S DIRECTIONS. RETURN TO THE START AND TURN TO PAGE 45.

You turn left, and the path immediately twists to your right. You walk for a bit and it twists to the left. At the end of this corridor, it turns right and then left again.

The maze takes you back and forth several more times before you feel you might be getting somewhere. You make a right and walk for a bit, then another right. After another short walk, you make one more right. At the end of the corridor you can go right or keep going straight.

On the wall to your left, you notice a small *L* in permanent marker on one of the planks close to the ground.

> IF YOU GO FORWARD, TURN TO PAGE 45.
> IF YOU GO RIGHT, TURN TO PAGE 63.

You go forward, and after a short distance, the path twists to your left. You walk for a long time, and it twists to the left again. At the end of this corridor, it turns left, and then immediately left again.

Is this what the mysterious *L* meant? You're excited because this could mean you're on the right track!

At the end of this corridor, you turn right around a wall. This path takes you to a left around another wall.

The maze takes you back and forth in this fashion several more times before you reach an intersection. You can go left or right.

On the wall in front of you, there is a small *L* in permanent marker on one of the planks close to the ground.

➤ IF YOU GO LEFT, TURN TO PAGE 64.
➤ IF YOU GO RIGHT, TURN TO PAGE 45.

You turn right, and the path immediately twists to your right. You walk for a bit and it twists to the left. The passage turns you right, and then left again.

The maze takes you back and forth several more times. This feels very familiar. You make a right and walk for a bit, then another right. After another short walk, you make one more right. At the end of the corridor, you can go right or keep going straight.

On the wall to your left, you notice a small *L* in permanent marker on one of the planks close to the ground.

You are pretty sure you have looped right back to where you started. If you're correct, when you go forward, you will be back at the entrance of the maze.

➤ GO FORWARD AND TURN TO PAGE 45.

You go left, and after a short distance, the path twists to your left. You walk for a long time, and it twists to the left again. At the end of this corridor, it turns left, and then immediately left again.

This seems so familiar.

You think, *There will be a right, then a left.* And sure enough, at the end of this corridor, you make a right around a wall. This path takes you to a left around another wall.

The maze takes you back and forth in this fashion several more times before you reach an intersection. You can go left or right. But the L on the wall in front of you tells you that you have probably just wasted your time. You'll know for sure if you turn right and end up back at the entrance to the maze.

➤ **GO RIGHT AND TURN TO PAGE 45.**

You are not going to let this place get to you. After all, it's just a game.

It's just a game, you repeat to yourself over and over as you walk along the path. It is definitely darker in this part of the maze. Maybe some of the lights burned out and they haven't replaced them.

Or maybe something disabled the lights on purpose.

They really overdid it on the vines and fog here. You can barely see your hand in front of your face.

The vines finally thin out and the fog lifts enough for you to make out the end of the corridor. A hulking figure is standing at the end of it.

Monty! You scream and back away. You try to turn and run, but you get tangled in the vines. You glance over your shoulder, expecting to see him coming for you, but he hasn't budged.

Monty doesn't move. In fact, he's smiling and pointing to his right.

Is he helping you? Maybe this is part of the VIP treatment.

You untangle yourself and slowly approach Monty, not wanting to make any sudden movements. You laugh when you get close enough to recognize that it's a cardboard cutout of the animatronic in his rock star pose. There are passages to your left and right. The Monty cutout is pointing to your left.

➤ **IF YOU GO LEFT, TURN TO PAGE 66.**
➤ **IF YOU GO RIGHT, TURN TO PAGE 67.**

Don't lead me the wrong way, you think as you follow cardboard Monty's direction.

The corridor is short and turns to the right. When you round the corner, you see another cardboard cutout of Monty Gator.

"Hey, little guy." He grins, showing his wicked sharp teeth.

Oh no! It's the real Monty!

"I can't believe you fell for that," he says, advancing toward you. "Run, run, run!"

➤ IF YOU RUN, TURN TO PAGE 59.

➤ IF YOU HAVE <u>CANDY</u>, TOSS IT AT MONTY AND TURN TO PAGE 60.

You know a trap when you see one, so you ignore cardboard Monty's helpful advice and head to your right. But you soon start to wonder if you made the correct choice. As you move down the passage, heavy footsteps follow you, closing in fast.

"Where're you going?" Monty calls out.

You reach an intersection and make a right, hurrying along and hoping you've thrown Monty off your trail. You reach another split path, but his growling comes from your right so you turn left.

And so it goes. On and on. You are being hunted, you're hopelessly lost, and it's only a matter of time before Monty catches up to you.

"VIP," you whisper. "Help?"

"Oh, now you remember me!" he says loudly.

"Shhhh!" You turn the volume down on the gamepad and press yourself against the wall. Heavy breathing is audible on the other side. *Oh no.*

"Listen closely and follow my directions for once," VIP says more softly. "I will lead you back to the entrance. Just go slowly and quietly so Monty does not get you first."

"Can I trust you?" you ask.

"You want to ask *him* instead? Devon, I want this game to go on for a long time, so it is in your best interest to trust me. And the best interest of your brother." A photo of your brother appears onscreen. You know that face: He's been crying.

➤ **FOLLOW VIP'S DIRECTIONS. RETURN TO THE START AND TURN TO PAGE 45.**

The next time you stumble back into the seven-path intersection, you pick a new direction and drop a tortilla chip at the start of the corridor. You drop another one each time you have a choice of direction. It's working! You get back to the intersection and see your chip lying in the fake grass across from you.

This maze is definitely looping you around, but you'll be able to find the correct route by the process of elimination. You drop another chip at a new path and continue on, feeling like you've finally got this labyrinth beat.

You reach a new seven-path intersection, and you're certain that it must be a different one because there are no chips on the ground.

Then you hear crunching from inside one of the corridors. You peek around the corner and see Monty there, delicately popping another tortilla chip into his gaping maw.

Yikes!

You think he hasn't seen you, but he says, "Thanks for the appetizer, kid."

Appetizer? Does that mean *you're* the main course?

You dump the rest of the chips on the ground, hoping it will distract him long enough for you to get away. And you run!

But you don't know where you're running to, and there's a good chance you will just bump into Monty again.

"A little help, VIP?" you ask.

"Certainly, Devon." VIP gives you a smug look. "I will guide you back to the start. Hurry."

➤ **RETURN TO THE START AND TURN TO PAGE 45.**

You reach into your pocket and pull out the package of Bonnie Bites you won from the Chica Candy Crane machine. The candy is warm and mushy now, but you hope Monty isn't a picky eater.

"Incoming!" you call as you throw the package at him.

Monty snaps his jaws at the bag and catches it in his teeth. He chews.

"Mph!" he mumbles. "Uh hehd deez!" He tries to open his mouth but it's cemented closed. He starts gagging and clawing at his snout. He pries open his jaw and you see sticky brown-and-purple goo sticking to his teeth. He reaches in to grab it, but one hand gets stuck inside.

He manages to free his hand but stumbles to the side and catches himself with his hand—and now his hand is stuck to the wall.

You can't help but laugh. But that makes Monty even angrier.

"Aaaaargh!" he roars. "Uhm gunnah ged chew!"

His tail thrashes and he swings his free arm wildly, grasping for you. If you're quick, you think you can slip past him to go down the left corridor. Or you can still head right, and you'll have a head start on him.

- **REMOVE <u>CANDY</u> FROM YOUR INVENTORY.**
- **IF YOU SLIP PAST MONTY AND GO LEFT, TURN TO PAGE 56.**
- **IF YOU GO RIGHT, TURN TO PAGE 55.**

There are two other kids in the Roxy Raceway pit area putting on silver helmets with green stripes down the center and gray wolf ears. You grab one for yourself and put down your gamepad.

"Since you have not been to Roxy Raceway before, it would be wise for you to listen to my go-karting tips," VIP says. He drives back and forth across the screen in the cartoon kart from the ads all over the Pizzaplex.

"You heard the guy at the door. I'm not allowed to bring you with me. Rules are rules," you say.

"Yes, rules are rules," VIP agrees.

➤ IF YOU LEAVE VIP BEHIND DURING YOUR RACE, TURN TO PAGE 71.
➤ IF YOU SNEAK VIP INTO YOUR GO-KART, TURN TO PAGE 72.

You leave the gamepad with the Pizzaplex employee in the pit area and look over your go-kart options. Only three types of go-karts are on the track and ready to go: a silver-and-purple one, a pink-and-white one, and a blue-and-red one.

You overhear one of the other kids say to his friend, "All the go-karts are supposed to be the same, but they aren't. Roxy's go-kart is the fastest."

You run ahead and cut him off before he can get into the silver-and-purple go-kart, climbing into it yourself. He shoots you an ugly look, and you shrug. The girl with him shakes her head as they move to the other two go-karts.

You buckle in and examine the controls before the race begins. Steering wheel, check. Accelerator, check. Brakes, check. "Turbo" button, check.

You aren't ready for how fast the go-kart is and scrape the wall as soon as you come out of the gate. You struggle to steer it, but you don't need to worry about keeping up: The other two racers don't seem to be interested in winning, only in getting in your way. They drive side by side and keep moving to block you. You're stuck behind them the whole way. You come in third place and collect VIP.

"Better luck tomorrow," VIP says.

"Tomorrow? What do you mean?"

"You broke *my* rule. You did not keep me with you. So, you can try to save Ike again tomorrow."

GAME OVER

➤ TO TRY AGAIN, TURN TO PAGE 2.

"I'm not leaving you behind." You strap on your helmet and pick up the gamepad.

VIP looks genuinely touched. "Thank you. You will not regret it."

Fortunately, the employees in the pit area aren't paying much attention to you so they probably won't notice you sneaking the gamepad into the go-kart.

"So how do I win this?" you ask, walking over to the track.

"Be the tortoise," VIP says.

"What is that supposed to mean?"

"I cannot do everything for you. I want you to win, but you have to earn it. That will be more fun. For both of us."

Grumbling, you consider your go-kart options. A tall white boy with long hair has already claimed the silver-and-purple go-kart, which you assume is based on Roxy. A short brown girl is mulling over the other two choices: a pink-and-white one, Glamrock Chica's colors, and a blue-and-red one, for Glamrock Bonnie.

Is there even a Glamrock tortoise?

"First time?" the girl asks.

You nod.

"Then you pick first. I don't care which one I drive."

"Thanks."

In the first row, the Chica go-kart is in first place. The Bonnie go-kart is in the second row in second place. The already claimed Roxy car brings up the rear.

"Are they all the same?" you ask.

"Supposedly," she says. "But I swear the Roxy go-kart is fastest."

➤ IF YOU PICK THE CHICA GO-KART, TURN TO PAGE 73.
➤ IF YOU PICK THE BONNIE GO-KART, TURN TO PAGE 74.

You climb into the pink-and-white go-kart. The girl gives you a thumbs-up and hops into the Bonnie go-kart to your right. You look around for someplace to stow the gamepad and are surprised to see a mount for it in the dashboard.

VIP waves his wand, and a map of the racecourse appears on the screen. "Since you only have one chance to win the game, this should give you a small advantage. The race consists of six laps."

You trace the path of the track around the Atrium. It has several hairpin turns and even crosses over the space a couple times.

"Is it safe to go over the Atrium like that?" you ask.

"We have not had any incidents yet," VIP says. "These race cars are thoroughly tested, however."

Roxanne Wolf's voice echoes overhead, "On your marks, get set, go!" A green light flashes, and you hit the accelerator.

It's strange driving so low to the ground, and 25 miles an hour is faster than you expected. You take it easy on the first lap to get a feel for the controls. Your opponents quickly zoom out of sight while you're learning how to turn without crashing.

You notice a "Turbo" button on the console. Maybe you should use it to make up time on the second lap.

> IF YOU PUSH THE "TURBO" BUTTON, TURN TO PAGE 75.
> IF YOU MAINTAIN YOUR SPEED, TURN TO PAGE 76.

You climb into the blue-and-red go-kart. The girl salutes you and hops into the Chica go-kart to your left. You look around for someplace safe to store the gamepad and find a mount for it in the dashboard.

VIP waves his wand, and a map of the racecourse appears on the screen. "Since you only have one chance to win the game, this should give you a small advantage. The race consists of six laps."

You trace the path of the track around the Atrium. It has several hairpin turns and even crosses over the space a couple of times.

"Wouldn't it be safer if the go-kart track was enclosed?" you ask.

"Research does suggest that is the case," VIP says.

Roxanne Wolf's voice echoes overhead, "On your marks, get set, go!" A green light flashes, and you pump the throttle.

It's strange driving so low to the ground, and 25 miles an hour is faster than you expected. You take it easy on the first lap while you're learning how to turn without crashing. But your go-kart is fast enough that you're able to keep pace between your two opponents, with the Roxy go-kart ahead and Chica trailing just behind you.

There's a "Turbo" button on the console. You'd like to see what this go-kart can really do when you give it everything it's got.

> **IF YOU PUSH THE "TURBO" BUTTON, TURN TO PAGE 84.**
> **IF YOU MAINTAIN THIS SPEED, TURN TO PAGE 85.**

You press the "Turbo" button and your go-kart rumbles. You press the throttle pedal with your right foot and accelerate beyond 25 mph, the previous top speed. Now it's 30 . . . 35 . . . You hit 45 mph and the go-kart feels like it's going to fly apart.

"Whoa!" VIP says, holding onto his top hat as though it's about to fly off. "This is a choice!"

Your wheels scrape the right wall and sparks fly, so you yank the steering wheel to the left. It shoots off away from the wall, and you twist the wheel back to the right to stabilize it. The go-kart's shaking back and forth now.

A turn is coming up fast!

➤ IF YOU HIT THE BRAKES WITH YOUR LEFT FOOT, TURN TO PAGE 77.
➤ IF YOU LIFT YOUR RIGHT FOOT FROM THE THROTTLE, TURN TO PAGE 78.

You can barely handle your go-kart at normal speed, so it's probably a bad idea to speed up just yet. You take the second lap faster than the first, so you feel like you're getting the hang of this. But you're still lagging behind the others and you wonder what else you can do to shave time off your laps.

It's only on the third lap when you're much more familiar with the course that you feel you can pay more attention to what your opponents are doing.

The boy in the Roxy go-kart has a comfortable lead. Counter to what you would expect, just before taking a turn, he steers his go-kart as close to the barrier on his right as he can without touching it. Then he cuts toward the inside of the track and lightly brakes as he goes into the turn. He ends up going wide again, traveling across the entire track, and comes out of it.

In contrast, the girl in the Bonnie go-kart does what you've been trying to do: cut close to the corners going as fast as possible, braking in the turn. Since it's a shorter distance to travel, it must be faster. This approach seems to work for her—she's only slightly behind the first racer. You just need to nail the timing and trajectory.

> ➤ IF YOU TRY GOING WIDER ON TURNS, TURN TO PAGE 80.
> ➤ IF YOU KEEP TAKING CORNERS FAST, TURN TO PAGE 81.

You slam on the brakes with your left foot as the turn comes up. You hear a horrible grinding noise and smell burning rubber. The back wheels lock and the front of your go-kart drifts to your left.

People outside El Chip's scream as you tear past, and you glimpse horrified faces as they drop to the ground and look for cover.

"Let up the throttle!" VIP says.

You lift your right foot from the accelerator and the go-kart straightens as you pull it out of the turn. You bring it to a full stop on the edge of the track. The Roxy and Bonnie go-karts zoom past on your left. The girl glances back to make sure you're all right. You smile and wave.

Your heart pounds in your chest, but you test the throttle and the go-kart is still working.

"I do not recommend braking and accelerating at the same time," VIP says.

"Now you tell me," you say.

"Some things should be obvious."

You are much more timid as you complete the rest of your laps and come in last. A nice crowd has gathered to watch you limp around the raceway, and several people clap slowly and ironically for you at the finish line.

"No points for you," VIP says with a shrug.

➤ TURN TO PAGE 109.

You release the accelerator and spin the wheel into the turn a little late, barely clearing it and then going wide to the outside of the track. You squeeze the brakes slightly to avoid ramming into the barrier, twisting the wheel to get yourself even.

You hear gasps and realize that people around the Pizzaplex are watching you on the big screens suspended over the raceway.

"Don't worry, it's all part of the show!" you call out. You press the "Turbo" button again to reduce the speed back down to 25 mph. *That's enough of that*, you think.

➤ **TURN TO PAGE 79.**

You drive around the track more slowly, focusing on learning how to handle your go-kart better: when to start braking (just before the turn, not when you're already in it), where to aim for each turn, and how to take advantage of the entire track.

When you aren't worried about being faster than your opponents, it's actually enjoyable to coast along past the Fazcade, Monty's Maze, and Bonnie Bowl.

To your surprise, when you cross the finish line, you've ended up in second place, even though you were third across the finish line.

"It is not about who is fastest," VIP says. "It is how fast you complete each lap, and you steadily improved each time. Well done."

Your fellow racers come over and shake your hand.

"Wasn't that fun?" the girl asks.

"It was," you say.

"That's all that matters." She smiles.

You wonder if she threw the race so you would place second. A little kindness goes a long way. You'd already been planning to treat Ike better when you free him from VIP, but you could try harder to be a better person in general and try to help others more.

"Not bad for your first race," the boy says. "You'll do better next time."

"If there *is* a next time," VIP says. He plays a dramatic sting: *Dun dun dunnnnn!*

➤ ADD 100 POINTS TO YOUR SCORE.
➤ TURN TO PAGE 109.

You work on copying what the kid in the Roxy go-kart is doing, and it actually works! By adjusting the angle at which you approach the corners, you head into them faster and maintain that momentum as you widen your exit from the turn.

In another couple of laps, you are racing right behind him, side by side with the Bonnie go-kart. The boy in the Roxy go-kart looks back and is surprised to see the both of you right on his tail. He starts driving more erratically, either because he's panicking or because he's intentionally trying to make it harder for you to pass him.

Whatever the reason, he's losing speed and you're gaining on him. You think you can overtake him and get first place in the last lap.

> IF YOU TRY TO PASS HIM, TURN TO PAGE 82.
> IF YOU GIVE HIM SOME SPACE, TURN TO PAGE 83.

You've played enough go-kart racing video games and seen enough action movies to know that the best drivers always use drift around corners. You have no idea how to pull that off in a real-life go-kart, but your opponents aren't doing it, so you might have an edge if you can master it.

You spend the next lap experimenting at each corner, taking them tighter and tighter. You nearly lose control of your go-kart a few times, but eventually you figure it out. By taking the corner close and then letting up on the throttle and turning the steering wheel *just right*, you're able to slide into those hairpin turns like the pros.

Some people in the Atrium are watching the race, and they clap as you drift through another turn. The funny thing is, it doesn't feel like you're taking those corners any faster than before. In fact, your lap times are getting longer.

Drifting looks cool, but maybe there's a good reason why no one else is doing it.

➤ **TURN TO PAGE 79.**

You nudge your go-kart forward and bump the back of the Roxy go-kart—just a warning. The boy in the Roxy go-kart turns and glares daggers at you. He starts to creep to the inside of the track, right in front of you.

He turns around and realizes he's about to enter a turn, so he stops throttling and slams on his breaks, then yanks the wheel so he moves to the outside of the track, and out of your way—inadvertently cutting off the girl in the Bonnie go-kart.

You zoom ahead of both of them, finally gaining the lead.

"Yeah!" You whoop with joy.

You finish the last lap in first place, closely followed by the Roxy go-kart and Bonnie go-kart, tied for second place.

So you're shocked when the scores appear on the big screen in the pit area and you have placed second overall. Then you see the lap times and you understand. Aside from the last lap, you were the slowest and honestly probably should have placed last.

➤ **ADD 100 POINTS TO YOUR SCORE.**
➤ **TURN TO PAGE 109.**

It feels too risky to try to pass the Roxy go-kart the way it's veering left and right unpredictably. So you back off and give him and the other car some space, prepared to ride this out and get a decent time regardless.

But the girl in the Bonnie go-kart sees an opening and she decides to make a move. She squeezes past on the boy's right, between him and the barrier . . . just as he sets himself up for another turn by steering toward the outside track.

They collide and smash into the barrier. The Roxy go-kart spins out and the Bonnie go-kart just locks up and grinds to a halt.

The crowd around the track gasps.

As you zip by your opponents, you glance over to make sure they're all right. They're in better shape than their go-karts, anyway. The girl waves you on.

Whew.

"Man. What happened?" you wonder aloud as you complete the lap.

"Two bodies cannot occupy the same space at the same time," VIP says. "An object in motion stays in motion. The laws of physics hold many harsh truths."

You cross the finish line and see that you are not only in first place, but you had the fastest overall lap times.

➤ **TURN TO PAGE 110.**

You press the "Turbo" button and your go-kart rumbles. You press the throttle pedal with your right foot and accelerate beyond 25 mph, the previous top speed. Now it's 30 . . . 35 . . . You hit 45 mph and the go-kart feels like it's going to fly apart.

Something pops in the engine behind you and you smell smoke and something . . . spicy? You lose control of the go-kart but fortunately it soon splutters to a halt. You look back and see splatters of green fluid in your wake.

Just like that, you're out of the race.

"What happened?" you ask VIP. "What's that green stuff?"

"Analysis identifies it as Monty Mystery Mix, available from various—"

"But what is it? What's in it?"

VIP adjusts his glasses. "You have asked questions even I cannot answer."

"Well, who would want to sabotage me?" You look at your opponents zipping by on the racetrack. You don't think the girl had anything to do with this, since she let you choose your go-kart first. Unless both of them had their Turbo button booby-trapped.

"It seems more likely that someone targeted that specific go-kart rather than a particular driver. Bad luck, Devon. Zero points awarded," VIP says.

"That's not fair. It's not my fault!"

"I did tell you not to choose that go-kart."

"Did you?"

"It was implied. Bonnie is a bunny, also known as a hare . . ."

You furrow your brow in confusion.

VIP shakes his head. "Read a book!"

➤ **TURN TO PAGE 109.**

As much as you'd like to leave everyone in your dust, you know you'd end up flying off the track into a birthday party or something if you turn up the juice. You're doing fine without Turbo anyway. Your lap times are improving, and you're still ahead of the girl in the Chica go-kart.

You keep glancing over your shoulder at her worriedly as she closes the distance on you. Finally, the two of you are bumper to bumper.

"Keep your eyes on the track ahead," she calls.

"What?" you ask, turning to look at her.

"The opposite of what you're doing. Face forward! Look ahead, not back, and not at the front of your go-kart. See? Every time you look at me, you slow down."

She's right. You focus your gaze on the course in front of you.

"Don't steer so much. Just nudge the wheel a little," she says. You make the adjustments and she's helpful again. You wish you were hanging out with her today instead of a Very Insulting Pig. "Better!"

Satisfied that you're making progress, she is clearly ready to pass you.

➤ IF YOU BLOCK HER FROM PASSING, TURN TO PAGE 86.
➤ IF YOU GET OUT OF HER WAY, TURN TO PAGE 87.

As she zooms up on your left, you say, "Not so fast!" and steer into her path. Your front left wheel bumps against her front right wheel, and the next thing you know, she isn't there anymore.

You look over your shoulder and see her go-kart spin out and smash into the barrier.

Oh no.

A couple laps later you slow down and watch as the girl is carried off the track and away on a stretcher by Pizzaplex paramedics.

When you cross the finish line, the boy from Roxy's go-kart is waiting for you.

"Way to go, dude. You got second place. I hope it was worth it," he says.

You feel terrible, but you just have to get Ike back. No matter what.

➤ **ADD 100 POINTS TO YOUR SCORE.**
➤ **TURN TO PAGE 109.**

As she zooms up on your left, you edge out of her way, right up to the barrier. You're on a straightaway, so she drives alongside you for a moment.

"Why are you helping me?" you ask.

"You're welcome." She laughs. "I love go-karting and I just want other people to enjoy it as much as I do. Is that so surprising?"

You feel terrible. Her words make you realize you hardly ever think about other people's happiness, only about how to get what you want. You didn't want to share your VIP pass with Ike, even though you knew how much he wanted to come to the Pizzaplex and meet Chica.

And then you abandoned him. This is all your fault.

Lost in thought, you've slowed down a bit, but you're close enough to the Chica go-kart to study how she is pushing it so fast. It all seems to be in the approach to the curves in the course and impeccable timing of braking and turning. You're not sure you'll ever get the feel for it—and you're unlikely to master it over the few remaining laps.

In lap five, you get your chance to place in the race, though. The Roxy go-kart is driving erratically to try to prevent the Chica go-kart from getting ahead. As the boy steers left to block the girl, you see an opening to pass him.

> IF YOU MAKE YOUR MOVE, TURN TO PAGE 88.
> IF YOU GIVE THEM SOME SPACE, TURN TO PAGE 89.

"You got it!" the girl cheers you on. "And stop leaning into your turns! Lean out!"

The boy cries out in frustration when your go-kart slips by him. He tries to ram into you from the left, but you slam the throttle and burst ahead, leaving him to scrape against the barrier and lose even more speed. And more of his temper.

He pursues you relentlessly around and around the course, over the arch midway that passes over the Play Area with the merry-go-round where you lost Ike.

I'm coming, bro, you think.

As you make those last tight turns in the final lap, you lean out like the girl suggested, and you feel your go-kart going faster as your weight shifts to the outside wheels. *Thanks again*, you think, pulling even farther ahead of the boy in what's supposed to be the fastest go-kart on the track.

You laugh with sheer exhilaration as you cross the finish line in second place!

You tumble out of your go-kart in the pit area and rush over to the girl. You offer a hand, and she shakes it.

"Thank you," you say. "I couldn't have done it without your help."

"What am I? Chopped pork?" VIP says, wearing a white chef's hat and apron that says EAT ME.

➤ **ADD 100 POINTS TO YOUR SCORE.**
➤ **TURN TO PAGE 109.**

It feels risky to attempt to pass the Roxy go-kart the way it's veering left and right unpredictably. So you slow down and ignore the other two cars, in favor of finishing the race with the best time you can manage.

"Are you even trying to win?" VIP asks.

"I'm learning," you say. "And I'm gradually getting better."

"I always support learning, but you could pick things up a bit. Or not. Depends on how much you want to get your brother back."

"Slow and steady wins the race, right?"

When you cross the finish line in third place, VIP says, "Unfortunately, in *this* story, you are the hare. Zero points."

➤ **TURN TO PAGE 109.**

The elevator lets you out into a narrow hallway with green-and-purple neon lights running along the walls and ceiling. You're surrounded by glowing stars, and the purple carpeting is adorned with ringed planets.

As you cross the hallway to the lobby, the speakers play Glamrock Freddy's voice: "Welcome! In this customized Fazer Blast Challenge, you will take on the role of an alien invading a space colony defended by none other than Freddy Fazbear himself. Hey, that is me!"

"He is such a ham," VIP says.

"Shhh! I want to listen to this," you say.

Freddy's announcement continues: "Soon you will be fighting for your life on a hostile planet. But in case you need to know how to play Fazer Blast or want a refresher, remember these two rules. Number one: No climbing; no jumping; no hitting, kicking, pushing, shoving; no shooting Fazerblasters in or close to other players' eyes. Being flashed in the eyes may induce seizures, blindness, or semipermanent paralysis. If you are flashed in the eyes, immediately flush your eyes with soap or water and blink repeatedly until vision is restored. Rule number two: Have fun. Proceed to the armory and suit up."

➤ TURN TO PAGE 91.

VIP

You reach the end of the corridor and find a small room filled with orange-and-blue tactical vests emblazoned with a bow tie and lightning bolt. There are helmets with bear ears on one side and helmets with deely boppers on the opposite side.

You're supposed to be the alien, so you grab the latter, slip on a matching vest, and grab a laser gun. The weapon is gunmetal gray with a fin on top of the barrel and a grille on the bottom. The tip of the gun has a golden glow, matching the illuminated lightning bolt on the grip.

"While you wait for the match to start, you may practice using the Fazerblaster in the shooting gallery," says Freddy's disembodied voice.

> IF YOU PRACTICE SHOOTING TARGETS, TURN TO PAGE 92.
> IF YOU JUST WAIT FOR FREDDY, TURN TO PAGE 93.

You head over to the gallery where a video screen shows a sepia-toned diorama of a party room with tables and a stage. The tables are covered with wrapped birthday presents and cone-shaped hats, while classic Freddy Fazbear and Bonnie the Bunny animatronics perform on a small stage in the back.

You practice shooting green-and-white bull's-eye targets that pop up throughout the room and zap green balloons floating across it. A counter in the corner of the screen shows the number of objects you hit and miss. As you play, your accuracy slowly improves to 98 percent.

"You are pretty good at that," VIP says. "But this is just a game. The real thing will be much more intense."

"Isn't this all just a game?" you ask.

"Perhaps," VIP says.

Music begins to play. It sounds familiar, but you can't quite place it.

"VIP, what is that song?"

"It is the Toreador Song, often known as the Toreador March, composed by George Bizet in 1875 for the French Opera *Carmen*."

"Why is it playing?" you ask.

"Freddy is here." VIP runs off screen.

➤ TURN TO PAGE 93.

The speakers pipe classical music. "Freddy Fazbear has entered the arena," says Freddy's recorded voice. "Prepare to play the sport of kings!"

"Laser tag is the sport of kings?" you ask.

"Report to the blue hallway," the voice continues. "Good luck!"

You take the doorway on the right and move through the blue hallway. You emerge into a wide-open space with low partitions.

Oh good, a maze, you think.

In each section you can see, the walls glow with a different color that pulsates from bright to dim: red and green on the lower level, purple above you. Ramps lead up to the purple area. You should be able to see the whole arena from up there, and get a sense of where the flags are—and where Freddy is.

➤ IF YOU TAKE THE HIGH GROUND, TURN TO PAGE 94.
➤ IF YOU TAKE THE LOW GROUND, TURN TO PAGE 95.

From the purple area on the upper level of the arena, you can clearly see two of the flags you need to capture below, one in the red section and one in the green.

Freddy has already claimed the green flag and is lingering nearby to defend it.

The third flag must be in the purple section up here and seems like the easiest target.

> IF YOU GO FOR THE PURPLE FLAG, TURN TO PAGE 98.
> IF YOU GO FOR THE RED FLAG, TURN TO PAGE 99.

You love playing first-person shooters, which is why you've been so eager to test your skills with "the real thing." You figure some of the best strategies apply here: stay low and keep moving.

So you stay low and keep moving as you make your way through the green area. The pulsating lights are disorienting, but you keep your head high, listening and watching. Freddy's heavy footsteps thump around nearby. That's one tactical advantage you have at least: You can sneak around silently, but he can't.

However, Freddy knows this arena better than you, and he's played this game before. As an animatronic with enhanced vision, you bet he's also a better shot than you.

You happen across a clearing with a flag on a podium beyond two low barriers. You press against a wall and peer around it to check out the situation. You don't hear anything. To capture that flag, you will have to push a button on the podium, which will likely sound an alert that brings Freddy straight to you.

Better be fast, you think.

You crouch run toward the flag, but you hear Freddy shout, "Freeze, alien scum! No offense, Devon."

➤ IF YOU HAVE A BALLOON, TURN TO PAGE 96.
➤ IF YOU DON'T HAVE A BALLOON, TURN TO PAGE 97.

Freddy seems strangely mesmerized by the balloon still tied to your wrist. You realize he must have been following it through the maze but not necessarily connecting it to your presence. Because of the light fluctuating from green to red to purple in the arena, the purple balloon seems to appear and disappear, which made it more difficult to track.

You rip it off your wrist and send it sailing up into the air. Freddy aims his Fazerblaster and starts firing at the balloon. It pops and confetti drifts down. But you're already sneaking away. While he was distracted, you darted back into the maze. Now, without the balloon, he won't be able to find you so quickly. Just to put some distance between you and get a better lay of the land, you slip up a ramp to the upper level.

➤ REMOVE BALLOON FROM YOUR INVENTORY.
➤ TURN TO PAGE 94.

VIP

You keep running toward the podium while Freddy fires his Fazerblaster at you. You dive behind one of the barriers, panting. Then you look down and notice that the bow tie and lightning bolt on the front of your vest are flashing red.

"I got you," Freddy says.

You step out from behind the barrier, head down.

"Do not be sad. You may have another chance to beat me one day. There is no shame in losing, only in giving up."

Freddy leads you to an elevator, which takes you back down to the Atrium, beside the entrance to Fazer Blast.

> ADD 100 POINTS TO YOUR SCORE.
> IF YOU HAVE NO MORE FAZ-TOKENS, TURN TO PAGE 106.
> IF YOU HAVE 1,000 POINTS, TURN TO PAGE 103.
> IF YOU HAVE NOT YET DONE MONTY'S MAZE, TURN TO PAGE 38.
> IF YOU HAVE NOT YET DONE ROXY RACEWAY, TURN TO PAGE 40.
> IF YOU GO TO THE ARCADE GAME ALCOVE, TURN TO PAGE 41.

You move swiftly and silently through the purple area until you discover the purple flag. Then you scout out an escape route and practice it a couple of times before you press the button to capture the flag.

The alert sounds, summoning Freddy: "Blue team has captured the purple flag. Defend!"

But instead of defending this flag, you follow your preplanned escape route back down to the lower level. You make your way over to where you saw the red flag. You wait and listen, scanning the environment around you for the slightest sign of movement. Then you swoop in and smack the button to capture the flag.

"Blue team has captured the red flag. Defend your station!"

That should keep him busy, you think, bolting for the green flag. You duck behind the podium and try to make yourself as small as possible. Freddy runs into the clearing behind you.

➤ IF YOU DID TARGET PRACTICE IN THE ARMORY, TURN TO PAGE 113.
➤ IF YOU DID NOT, TURN TO PAGE 114.

You sneak back down to the lower level, thinking that Freddy may have seen you in the purple area and the coast is currently clear. You can hear his footsteps thumping on the astronaut-themed carpeting, showing line drawings of Freddy in a round glass helmet. But you can't tell what direction they're coming from or how close he is.

You make your way over to where you saw the red flag. You wait and listen, scanning the environment around you for the slightest sign of movement. Then you swoop in and smack the button to capture the flag.

An alert says, "Blue team has captured the red flag. Defend your station!"

You duck behind one of the barriers in front of the podium, trying to decide if you should run and try to grab the green flag as well before Freddy finds you.

Too late. Freddy has found you.

He fires at you and hits the barrier you're taking cover behind. He steps into view. You must act now!

➤ IF YOU DID TARGET PRACTICE IN THE ARMORY, TURN TO PAGE 111.
➤ IF YOU DID NOT, TURN TO PAGE 112.

VIP's Game Rules

Remember this page and come back to it whenever you need to!

1. Use Faz-Tokens to play games in the Pizzaplex.
2. Earn at least 1,000 points by the end of the day to save Ike.
3. You can only play each game once.
4. Ask VIP for help or suggestions while playing the game.
5. If you run out of Faz-Tokens before earning 1,000 points, you lose.

Keep good notes on the number of Faz-Tokens you have, the games you've played, your score, and any active game conditions.

➤ IF YOU RUN OUT OF TOKENS AND HAVE FEWER THAN 1,000 POINTS, TURN TO PAGE 106.
➤ IF YOU COLLECT 1,000 POINTS, TURN TO PAGE 103.
➤ WHEN YOU'RE READY TO BEGIN VIP'S CHALLENGE, RETURN TO THE ATRIUM AND TURN TO PAGE 26.

VIP

You like Virtual Informative Pig more than his know-it-all counterpart.

"While you're in the MOE, special conditions apply," he explains. "Your scores are multiplied by 10. So, 300 points times 10 would give you . . . ?"

You scratch your head.

"It's easy." On the gamepad he shows the number 300. "Just add an extra zero on the end." A zero rolls onto the screen from the right and crashes into the 300, making it 3,000.

"Wow!"

"VIP must honor this. The games may be simulated, but in the Pizzaplex, points are points. Also, when restarting the game, you can keep any points you have already earned. You now have all the Faz-Tokens you started with again, and all games you've already played are reset, so you can play them again."

"Sweet!"

"That is enough from you, Virtual Interfering Pig." The real VIP drops into the screen. He points his magic wand at his doppelganger. "Fazmagoria!"

Writhing purple energy emanates from the wand and swirls around the nicer VIP.

"Good luck, Devon . . ." Virtual Informative Pig's words fade with him.

"Now, get on with it," VIP says.

Make a note that **MOE Special Conditions** are in effect. Multiply any new points you acquire by 10.

If this is your second time or beyond in the MOE, make a note that **Double MOE Special Conditions** are in effect. Multiply any new points you acquire by 100.

You may keep your current points and replay any games you have already played. You may also keep any items in your inventory.

> IF YOU WANT TO EXPLORE THE FAZCADE, TURN TO PAGE 27.
> IF YOU WANT TO EXPLORE THE ATRIUM, TURN TO PAGE 28.
> IF YOU WANT TO EXPLORE ROCKSTAR ROW, TURN TO PAGE 31.

"Hey, VIP," you say gleefully. "I did it! I have a thousand points."

"Impossible!" he says.

"Surely, you knew how many points I've been collecting. Don't you know everything?"

VIP turns red and begins stomping around the screen. Sparks and fire spew from his magic wand. "I do not know how you did this! You must have cheated somehow."

"But you were there with me the whole time."

VIP calms down. "I apologize. I was just having such a good time with you, I did not want our time together to end."

You're starting to get nervous. "I would like to see my brother now, VIP. Please."

"Of course. A deal is a deal. Take me to the center of the Atrium."

You carry the gamepad over to the Play Area in the middle of the Atrium. The Pizzaplex is closing soon, and people are streaming toward the exits, looking exhausted but happy.

VIP makes a complicated gesture in the air with his magic wand that you're pretty sure is all just for show, and the door to the photobooth pops open. Ike comes tearing out and makes a beeline for you.

"Hey, buddy." You kneel and wrap him in your arms. Ike snuggles up against you. He does give good snuggles, you admit. "I'm sorry, bro."

➤ TURN TO PAGE 115.

You stand outside the VIP Greeting Room's nondescript door and bang on it with a fist. "Little pig, little pig! Let me in!"

"D-d-do you have one-hundred thousand points already?" VIP asks on your gamepad. Why is he so nervous?

"I sure do," you say.

"Then no need to huff and puff." He sighs. "A deal is a deal . . ." He walks off the gamepad screen and the door unlocks.

You're in a server closet with racks of computer hard drives blinking and clicking and flashing and whirring. And in the center of it all, a large screen hovers with VIP's face on it.

So pigs do fly, you think.

"Is this some kind of *Wizard of Oz* thing?" you ask.

"Wh-wh-what do you want?" VIP's little rotors buzz, and he pulls up and away from you, bumping against the machine banks at the back of the small room.

"I wanted to meet you in person, or whatever this is."

"Thank you for a fun day, Devon. I will let Ike go now, of course."

"You bet you will. And this ends. You won't ever do this again."

"Yes! I p-p-promise."

"Your 'piggy promise' doesn't mean anything to me," you say.

"Please don't hurt me!" VIP wails. His screen spins and weaves around the room. You shut the door behind you before he can escape.

➤ **TURN TO PAGE 116.**

VIP

It feels strange to put on Freddy's head, but once the helmet settles into place, it's rather cozy and smells like a brand-new car. You can see the terminal in front of you, but the mask's eyes must also be a screen because a heads-up display shows a full battery charge.

A pleasant male voice comes from speakers near your ears: "Thank you for choosing the MAX Occupancy Experience. We know you are disappointed that the Mega Pizzaplex has reached maximum capacity, or your favorite attraction is currently under construction, or unavoidable circumstances for which we cannot be held liable have temporarily disrupted available services."

You're beginning to have second thoughts about this. But before you can remove the helmet, the voice resumes.

"This high-quality re-creation of the Pizzaplex was designed to be indistinguishable from the real thing, and in some ways the MOE is even better: There is a very low chance of involuntary dismemberment or lobotomy. All food contains zero calories. And during your virtual visit, all games provide ten times their usual points, which still may be exchanged at the real prize center. Tap 'Start' to initialize the MOE."

A green button labeled "Start" floats in front of you. Below it is a red "Cancel" button.

Note that if you use the MOE, you must restart this game from the beginning. All game uses will be reset—you can keep current points and replay any games you have already played.

➤ IF YOU PRESS "START," TURN TO PAGE 43.
➤ IF YOU PRESS "CANCEL," TURN TO PAGE 44.

You reach into your pocket and come up empty. You are out of Faz-Tokens. Panic washes over you.

"VIP, I'm out of tokens." Your voice is thick with emotion, and when you blink, tears fall.

"Do you have a thousand points yet?" VIP asks.

"Not yet. Could I please have some more tokens?"

VIP considers. "Of course."

You can hardly believe your ears. "Really? That's amazing of you, VIP. Thank you!"

"You can have more tokens . . . tomorrow."

You swallow. "What do you mean?"

"Since you played along so well today, I will give you another chance to win my challenge tomorrow."

You shake your head. "But what about Ike? He can't last until then."

"I hope that you are wrong. For his sake."

"What will I tell our mother?"

"Oh, you cannot leave, either. We would not want you trying to bring help back to the Pizzaplex. No, if you leave, or call anyone for help, you will never find Ike. I can show you somewhere to hide until morning. Until you can beat me, you and your brother will just be another pair of mysteriously missing kids. It will not be the first time, and I dare say it will not be the last."

GAME OVER

➤ TO TRY AGAIN, TURN TO PAGE 2.

You've never been to a swamp before, but you aren't sure anyone at Fazbear Entertainment has, either. The floor is covered in rough artificial grass that reminds you more of miniature golf courses, and the lights are dim and very, very green. The lighting hangs from rigging high above you, along with more fake greenery: plants and vines. It looks like there's a catwalk up there, which is probably where staff watches guests in the maze.

It's incredibly hot and humid in here. Someone needs to fix the AC, you think as you wipe sweat from your face with one hand.

You move into the maze. The purple balloon you won from Balloon Boy's Balloon Dispenser bobs up and down as high as the wooden walls on either side of you. It brushes against the fronds of palm trees stretching overhead—also artificial.

You walk along the narrow corridor for a bit, feet crunching softly on the turf. The path turns to the right, then the left, and eventually you reach an intersection. You can continue forward, turn left, or turn right.

Before you can choose one, Monty Gator leaps into your path.

"Nice balloon, kid," he growls. "Made it simple to find you." The alligator animatronic winks behind his star-shaped shades, then slashes your balloon with vicious claws. It pops and releases confetti into the air.

"Aw, too bad. I'll show you out," he says.

> ADD 100 POINTS TO YOUR SCORE. REMOVE BALLOON FROM YOUR INVENTORY.
> TURN TO PAGE 107.

The exit dumps you back into the Atrium at a door you hadn't noticed previously, though now you see Monty's footprints on the patterned carpet leading into it.

- IF YOU HAVE NO MORE FAZ-TOKENS, TURN TO PAGE 106.
- IF YOU HAVE 1,000 POINTS, TURN TO PAGE 103.
- IF YOU HAVE NOT YET DONE FAZER BLAST, TURN TO PAGE 39.
- IF YOU HAVE NOT YET DONE ROXY RACEWAY, TURN TO PAGE 40.
- IF YOU GO TO THE ARCADE GAME ALCOVE, TURN TO PAGE 41.

VIP

Your legs are shaky as you climb out of your go-kart, drop your helmet at the desk, and stagger out to the Atrium the same way you came in. Your whole body feels numb. You can't believe you survived that! You're glad you don't have to drive around the Atrium again today. You would much rather walk.

- IF YOU HAVE NO MORE FAZ-TOKENS, TURN TO PAGE 106.
- IF YOU HAVE 1,000 POINTS, TURN TO PAGE 103.
- IF YOU HAVE NOT YET DONE MONTY'S MAZE, TURN TO PAGE 38.
- IF YOU HAVE NOT YET DONE FAZER BLAST, TURN TO PAGE 39.
- IF YOU GO TO THE ARCADE GAME ALCOVE, TURN TO PAGE 41.

You steer your go-kart over to the pit and see Roxanne Wolf waiting for you. The slender animatronic seems even taller from the low go-kart. You look up, taking in her purple leg warmers, red shorts, and black racing jacket. She brushes back the green streak in her silver hair and gazes at you with piercing yellow eyes.

"That was a ferocious performance." Roxy reaches a large, gray hand (or paw?) down. You take it, the metal cold and hard against your fragile human flesh, and she easily lifts you out of your go-kart.

She kicks a tire of the go-kart. "Chica fanboy?" She sounds disappointed.

"My little brother is."

She walks you back out to the Atrium.

"Want an autograph?" she asks.

"I'd love one."

She pulls out a glossy photograph of herself playing a green keytar on stage and scribbles on it. Then she leaves to prepare for the next Glamrock show.

You read her message: FROM ONE WINNER TO ANOTHER. GOOD LUCK FINDING YOUR BROTHER. ROXY.

➤ ADD 300 POINTS TO YOUR SCORE. ADD ROXY'S AUTOGRAPH TO YOUR INVENTORY.
➤ IF YOU HAVE NO MORE FAZ-TOKENS, TURN TO PAGE 106.
➤ IF YOU HAVE 1,000 POINTS, TURN TO PAGE 103.
➤ IF YOU HAVE NOT YET DONE MONTY'S MAZE, TURN TO PAGE 38.
➤ IF YOU HAVE NOT YET DONE FAZER BLAST, TURN TO PAGE 39.
➤ IF YOU GO TO THE ARCADE GAME ALCOVE, TURN TO PAGE 41.

You aim your Fazerblaster at the target on Freddy's chest and fire. The tip of your laser pistol lights up, and sparks fly from Freddy. Direct hit!

You jump out from behind the barrier and rush over to Freddy.

"Do not worry about me," Freddy says. "I am fine. Fazerrific shooting, Devon."

Freddy leads you to the winner elevator, which takes you back down to the Atrium, beside the entrance to Fazer Blast.

- ADD 100 POINTS TO YOUR SCORE.
- IF YOU HAVE NO MORE FAZ-TOKENS, TURN TO PAGE 106.
- IF YOU HAVE 1,000 POINTS, TURN TO PAGE 103.
- IF YOU HAVE NOT YET DONE MONTY'S MAZE, TURN TO PAGE 38.
- IF YOU HAVE NOT YET DONE ROXY RACEWAY, TURN TO PAGE 40.
- IF YOU GO TO THE ARCADE GAME ALCOVE, TURN TO PAGE 41.

You shoot . . . and you miss!

But Freddy gets a direct hit on the target on your chest. The bow tie and lightning bolt on your vest flash red, indicating that you're out of the game.

"It seems you could use more practice," Freddy says. "But I am certain you will be able to beat me next time. Thank you for playing."

Freddy takes you to an elevator that brings you back down to the Atrium, beside the entrance to Fazer Blast.

- ADD 100 POINTS TO YOUR SCORE.
- IF YOU HAVE NO MORE FAZ-TOKENS, TURN TO PAGE 106.
- IF YOU HAVE 1,000 POINTS, TURN TO PAGE 103.
- IF YOU HAVE NOT YET DONE MONTY'S MAZE, TURN TO PAGE 38.
- IF YOU HAVE NOT YET DONE ROXY RACEWAY, TURN TO PAGE 40.
- IF YOU GO TO THE ARCADE GAME ALCOVE, TURN TO PAGE 41.

You lean out from behind the podium and smack the button to claim the green flag, at the same time that you fire your Fazerblaster at the target on Freddy's chest.

Bull's-eye!

Sparks fly from Freddy's vest. You get ready for some kind of tantrum or disappointment, but Freddy smiles.

"You win, superstar!" he says. "You exercised good strategy and skill, practicing and planning ahead. Are you sure you have not played Fazer Blast before?"

You nod your head.

"I hope we can play together again sometime. But I know you have other things to do for the rest of today's visit." Freddy eyes the VIP gamepad suspiciously. VIP is strangely hanging out somewhere offscreen.

"Hmm," Freddy says. "Be careful with that one."

He leads you to the winner's elevator and sees you off. It takes you back down to the Atrium.

➢ ADD 300 POINTS TO YOUR SCORE.
➢ IF YOU HAVE NO MORE FAZ-TOKENS, TURN TO PAGE 106.
➢ IF YOU HAVE 1,000 POINTS, TURN TO PAGE 103.
➢ IF YOU HAVE NOT YET DONE MONTY'S MAZE, TURN TO PAGE 38.
➢ IF YOU HAVE NOT YET DONE ROXY RACEWAY, TURN TO PAGE 40.
➢ IF YOU GO TO THE ARCADE GAME ALCOVE, TURN TO PAGE 41.

You pop out from behind the podium and fire at the target on Freddy's chest, but your shot goes wide and sparks fly from his eyes instead.

He flinches and rears his head back, body convulsing. You race toward him. "Freddy? Are you okay?" you scream.

He leans forward, then lurches upright, arms flailing. His hand smacks into your head and everything goes dark.

You come to in Freddy's arms at a health station in the Atrium. "I am so sorry, Devon. I do not know what came over me. I would never hurt you intentionally. None of the animatronics would. It goes against our programming."

You rub the big bump on your forehead. It aches something fierce, and you know it's going to leave a nasty bruise. Wait until you tell the kids at school that you got into a fight with Freddy Fazbear.

Nah, they'll never believe it.

"Too bad we did not finish our game," Freddy says. "I look forward to a rematch one day."

➤ IF YOU HAVE NO MORE FAZ-TOKENS, TURN TO PAGE 106.
➤ IF YOU HAVE 1,000 POINTS, TURN TO PAGE 103.
➤ IF YOU HAVE NOT YET DONE MONTY'S MAZE, TURN TO PAGE 38.
➤ IF YOU HAVE NOT YET DONE ROXY RACEWAY, TURN TO PAGE 40.
➤ IF YOU GO TO THE ARCADE GAME ALCOVE, TURN TO PAGE 41.

"S'okay," Ike says. He hands you a fistful of photo strips from the booth. You flip through them. In the first photos, he looks happy, making goofy expressions. Then he's red-faced and crying. As the images progress, they become a self-portrait of abject misery.

"I knew you would get me out," he says.

"Let's, um, not show all of these to Mom," you say.

"Can we go home now?" Ike asks.

"A hundred percent."

You walk the gamepad back to the checkout desk. You can't wait to get rid of VIP once and for all.

"This was everything I hoped it would be," VIP says. "I hope tomorrow is just as perfect."

You stop in your tracks. "Tomorrow?"

"Did you think you were the only one to get a VIP invitation?"

"Kind of."

"I mailed dozens of them. I can do this every day! Just think of it. So much fun to be had."

Oh no, you think. *What have I done?*

What can I do? You fear you have no choice but to get as far away from here as possible with your little brother, and never return. You realize even if you warned your friends not to come back, they wouldn't listen.

Now you have an idea what it's like to be VIP: Full of knowledge, but no one to share it with.

You hand the gamepad back to a Pizzaplex employee without meeting their eyes.

"How was your visit?" they ask.

"Very . . . informative."

You aren't quite sure how to end this. There's no keyboard in here, not that you know anything about computer programs. Maybe you can go get something to smash VIP's screen with——but you've seen him on other screens all over the Pizzaplex. It would be no more effective than destroying his gamepad.

You glance down at the gamepad and you see another VIP, even while he's still frantically flitting around your head. If you don't do something soon, he'll probably start to attack *you*. And there's only one Devon.

The small VIP on the gamepad takes a step and somehow duplicates himself. It's starting to become Pigception in here.

Oh, you realize. Those aren't the Very Informative Pigs. Those are Virtual Informative Pigs because you're still in the MOE. And they're pointing toward something along the wall. You walk with the gamepad and they adjust where they're pointing, as if you were holding a compass with the needle following north.

"Wh-wh-what are you d-d-doing?" the big VIP screams, "Get away from there!" His face starts to glitch, and you get a creepy glimpse of the wireframe behind his pink skin and glasses.

The pigs—Virtual Informative Pigs—your friends—are pointing at a massive power strip on the floor that has dozens of plugs in it, a tangle of cables.

You snap your fingers. Of course! You trace the main power plug to a wall outlet.

➤ TURN TO PAGE 116.

"This won't erase you?" you whisper to the Virtual Informative Pigs.

"We don't know," they say, and they seem delighted by the prospect of *not* knowing something.

"If we're part of the simulation, we may be running in a separate program," one of them says.

"But Pig Brother is also part of this simulation." They confer with one another, then they look up. "Everything is connected. What happens in here will affect the real world."

You nod. "Well, then. Thank you. And goodbye." You hope you won't meet any digital swine ever again.

You yank at the plug.

"Stooooooooopppp!" The big VIP screen wheels toward you, but before it can knock you away, the plug comes free. The outlet sparks and sizzles like bacon in a frying pan. The flying screen drops and cracks on the tiled floor. Snow dances across it and the gamepad's screen.

"It's over," you say.

Then the world around you starts to deteriorate, too. You reach up and tear off the MOE headset. Around you, everything is chaos in the Atrium. Every system seems to be down, every screen is dark.

Everything is connected.

People scream and run for the exits. You wonder if the animatronics have been affected by the forced system shutdown.

The photobooth door opens and Ike comes running out. He stands still in all the commotion, looking around in fear. You hurry over to him.

"Ike!" You grab him in your arms and Ike sobs. "I'm sorry."

➤ TURN TO PAGE 117.

"Let's go home," Ike says.

"I just have to do one more thing," you say.

On your way out of the Pizzaplex—likely for the last time—you stop at the Security Office and tell the gray-haired white guy there about what happened. The guard listens closely, nodding and taking notes.

"Well done, Devon," he says. "And Ike." You don't know if it's more worrying that he believed your outrageous story than if he had dismissed it as a prank or fantasy. "I always thought that pig might be trouble. He was very intrusive."

You couldn't agree more.

"Don't worry, Fazbear Entertainment will make all this go away like it never happened," he says. "And that especially includes VIP. This will just be our little secret, huh?"

"Okay. I don't think anyone else will believe me anyway." You look at Ike. "Especially Mom, right, bro?"

Ike nods. "When she asks how our day was, I'll just say it was . . . very informative."

And that's the truth.

ABOUT THE AUTHORS

SCOTT CAWTHON is the author of the bestselling video game series *Five Nights at Freddy's*, and while he is a game designer by trade, he is first and foremost a storyteller at heart. He is a graduate of The Art Institute of Houston and lives in Texas with his family.

E. C. MYERS was assembled in the United States from Korean and German parts and raised by a single mother and the public library in Yonkers, New York. He won the Andre Norton Nebula Award for his first novel, *Fair Coin* (2012), and is the author of *The Silence of Six* and the RWBY young adult books, including *After the Fall* (2019), *Fairy Tales of Remnant* (2020), and *Roman Holiday* (2021). His short fiction has been published in various anthologies, including *Tasting Light: Ten Science Fiction Stories to Rewire Your Perceptions*, *Mother of Invention*, and *A Thousand Beginnings and Endings*. He has also written for several serialized podcasts, including *The Sounds of Nightmares* (from the world of *Little Nightmares*) and *Orphan Black: The Next Chapter*.

A DEADLY SECRET IS LURKING AT THE HEART OF FREDDY FAZBEAR'S PIZZA...

Unravel the twisted mysteries behind the bestselling horror video games and the *New York Times* bestselling series.